MOLLY'S LAIRD

JOANNE AUSTEN BROWN

Molly's Laird

BOOKS BY JOANNE AUSTEN BROWN

Always Louisa ~ Book One: Always Series

Always Elspeth ~ Book Two: Always Series

Rachael's Jaunt ~ Book One: Come With Me

I dedicate this book to all the victims of the Ruby Princess. And to their families.

1

THAT STRANGE LIGHT

The teal blue light rested on the face of the woman, asleep on the Fairy Hill. She had been coming to the hill for a few weeks. A dark-haired beauty, obviously looking for solace or she was trouble. This woman had history and biology that disturbed him. But for now, he would keep his concerns to himself. He did not want to tell his queen he knew more than he was telling.

"She is here again. What are we to do?" Drake wandered over to her and kneeled in front of the sleeping beauty.

"We will send her back but not just yet. Molly has experienced a great deal of grief in a few short months. She needs more time to heal and then she will be ready."

"You are sure she is the right one for the laird? She seems so different to Rachael."

"She is. But then she is meant for the new laird not Duncan. We found his love. Now its Alasdair's turn."

"But even in this age she seems to be a fish out of water. She is beautiful but so unsure of herself. Can she really be ready for such a move? Can she believe the fae are true, let alone time travel?" Alvina walked over to him and placed her hand on his shoulder.

He stood.

"Can you not see the likeness? There is fairy blood in her. I thought as you but have pondered the future and the past with insight. She too, like Rachael, is important to the survival of our race. And the keeping of our kingdoms."

He looked down at the dark-haired miss. Asleep, she was resting in beauty. The fairy look was there. He could not deny it. The elements of part fairy and part human. Rachael did not have it but was a good choice for Duncan. Can a part fairy miss win the heart of a man who took so many years to come to believe in the facts about his own family? And then accept that she came to him because she too had fairy blood? Was she even aware of the connection? There were too many questions.

The Murray's were important to them. He knew that. But this woman? This grieving lady who had lost so much. Can she overcome all doubts and time to be the link for fairy existence? He knew who she really was.

Alvina, with a touch of her hand, turned him toward her.

"Do you trust me?"

"That is a ridiculous question. I would not be here if I did not trust and love you."

He looked into her magical eyes. Eyes that revealed all she had given him. Eyes that shone even in the dark. She was fae and he adored her.

Reaching out, she took him into her arms and kissed him. Tightening his arms around her, he deepened the kiss. This was such a rare experience. To kiss the queen away from the privacy of their inner sanctum. He loved this woman; this fairy queen more than he had loved anyone. And she was demonstrating that love for anyone who might be looking. And there was always someone looking.

He held her close and rested his forehead against her royal forehead. They held each other.

"Just let me know when." It could have been a hundred years from now for all he cared.

Finally, she pulled herself away and walked to the side of the hill and looked down on the village of Aberlour. He came and stood next to her. He turned to gaze at his queen.

"My dearest Drake, I do nothing without consulting you. This is our future. I need you. You are my rock. I love you."

"I know, your majesty, my light." Heat rose to his face.

She smiled at him, and her face radiated the love they shared. She took his hand. He would always love her. He needed to tell her the whole truth. Come what may.

The teal blue light faded, and the dark-haired lady continued to sleep.

2

WHY HAS THIS HAPPENED?

Fairy Hill, October 2020

Molly stretched and sat up. She had fallen asleep on the hill again. That was the fifth time. She stood up and walked over the edge of the hill and looked down on Aberlour, her new home at least for now. The timeless buildings resting in the early morning mist. She stretched again. She was refreshed, no bones ached. No headache. She wasn't even cold. Her heart, that had been so heavy to carry around, was lighter. Walking back to the rock, she picked up her backpack, and made her way down the hill and into the town. It was deserted as it had been for many weeks. Lockdown. Would it save her? She doubted it.

The occasional car passed her. But she was not concerned. The door of a house she passed would open. But just for a moment. The person might come out their door. They would wave but go back inside. She was okay. They were safe. She wore a mask. Black like her soul. The sun was shining at least for now. Clouds were gathering but that was usual in Scotland. Four seasons in one day. Reminded her of Melbourne.

After a few more minutes she arrived at Mrs. Watson's B & B. She opened the front door and went in.

"Is that you, Molly dear?"

"Yes Mrs. Watson."

"Remember dear, call me Aunty Jess."

"Sorry aunty. I forgot."

"Now come and have some breakfast. I take it you fell asleep on the hill?"

"Yep, I did. Again. That's five times now. I don't mean too. It just happens."

Leaving her backpack by the door she came and sat at the kitchen table. She rubbed her head and then gave it a little shake.

"Seems my body has a mind of its own."

"Ahh, my dear girl. You have been through a great deal of pain. The hill can detect your sorrow and probably helps you to sleep. You need to heal."

"I never thought I would say this but the fae, fairies, who own the place, seem to be real. I always feel better when I have spent a night up there. Fairies. Who would have thought?"

"Ah me deary. They are real. I could tell you stories..."

"Perhaps you should, tell me I mean. I think you could make me a believer right now."

"Well, that is a good thing, isn't it? Believing will help you heal too. Now here is some eggs and bacon and potato cakes."

Molly looked at the food, then at Mrs. Watson, aunty. She smiled at the dear lady who had taken her into her home and made her part of her own family. The fae was real to Aunty Jess. She believed in their healing powers. After all, how else could she explain all the strange things that had happened to her since she arrived here.

She had no one anymore. She took a deep breathe. In the space of six months, she had lost her mother, sister, and toddler niece. It was more than she could bear let alone think about. And the hill was the only place that gave her peace. She didn't understand it, but it was very real. That place had healing powers.

"Thanks aunty. This looks great. And I feel hungry." She jumped up and went to the kitchen sink and soaped and scrubbed her hands. Drying them, she turned to Mrs Watson.

"I thought you might. You have every time you have come down from the hill. Now eat up."

Molly sat down and poured a cuppa. Just like home. Nothing like a strong black cup of liquid with healing properties. No tea bags here. Just the real thing. Tea also had its healing power over her. Remembering all her tea parties with her mum didn't make her cry with pain anymore. It brought a smile to her face.

"I need to make a phone call but I *wilna* be long." Mrs. Watson left the room and walked down the hall to the landline phone that was on the wall. She heard muffled words and a few minutes later she was back.

"Oh, Aunty Jess, this food is glorious."

"That is high praise coming from you *deary*."

Molly again grinned at Mrs Watson. I guess high praise it might be, but it was true. She loved her cooking but relished when someone else cooked for her. Being a chef had opened so many doors for her. Not being able to cook right now, hurt her. It was part of who she was. It made her feel more alone than she could say. Cooking made her feel alive. So right now, she was on the verge of being lost completely. But was sure the hill would not let that happen. She would cook again but she was intent to wait till another time and place. She needed to heal. Mrs Watson, aunty, could cook for her and keep her sane.

After breakfast, she made her way upstairs to her bedroom. Mrs. Watson had been in and cleaned up for her. She went to the desk and could see that she had not cleaned up her thoughts. The papers, diaries and photos were there just as she had left them last evening. Journaling was helping her to remember all the good her life had experienced. And to manage the not so good experiences. It was cathartic.

She took off her clothes and placed them in the laundry basket in the bathroom. She hopped into the shower. Here in the quiet and the steam of the bathroom, tears streamed down her face. She cried for her sister Skye and niece Flora. They had been killed on January twenty-third, 2020, in a car accident.

This was fate.

Skye would have hated being in lockdown in Melbourne. Poor Melbourne had been in lockdown so long through this crazy year of 2020.

At least they went together.

The tears continued to fall and the water from the shower covered her face.

3

WHO ARE YOU?

Fairy Hill, July 1823

"I miss them both, Glenna. I know we have done the right thing. Me now, the laird and Duncan with Rachael. But I miss them."

She watched as he ran his fingers through his hair. He loved to walk around the estate not wearing a hat. And she had to agree it was a beautiful day to be hatless. She too enjoyed the breeze through her curls.

"I do understand, Dair. You need a mate, someone who can share your troubles with."

"Well, that is not going to happen. Is it? There is no one." She watched him lower his head and examine his feet as they continued their climb up the hill.

"Delia did have feelings for you."

"But she could not wait any longer. I do not blame her. I kept her on a string for five years."

"Actually, it was six."

Alasdair looked at her. He was not amused even though she

was right. He was questioning everything in his life and she, as his sister, could understand why he did. And she could pick his mood. He did not like to be corrected.

"Very well, six years. But it was right for her to go. I did not love her. Not real love. She needed romantic love. I could not give it to her."

"Why? She did have love for you."

"I know. And that is why I am glad she has gone home. I miss her company. But I did not love her in the romantic sense. She was like a sister to me. I think I might not be able to love anyone. Certainly not the kind of love Duncan has for Rachael. After watching their love bloom, I could see I lacked the ability. Perhaps being alone is my punishment for treating Rachael as I did."

"That is ridiculous, and you know it."

"I do not know anything anymore. I am questioning every aspect of my so-called life."

They continued to make their way to the top of Fairy Hill. They walked there nearly every day since Duncan had left. Glenna never expected Duncan to return but deep down she hoped both Duncan and Rachael would come back. They had not. They had chosen their life in the future. Now she wanted Alasdair to find his soulmate.

There seemed to be someone on the hill. Her heart was beating faster as she quickened her pace to the top. Who was there? A woman. Black flowing hair and a curved figure. But wearing the pants, jeans, Rachael called them, from the future. The woman turned around. She was beautiful.

Alasdair grabbed her hand as they reached the top. He pulled her back behind him.

He's still trying to protect his little sister.

"Glenna, is that you?" the woman asked.

"Who are you?" Dair spoke roughly, more than he normally would.

"I'm Molly. Molly Grace. Glenna? You must be Alasdair. Rachael said you would be wary."

"You know Rachael?" He took a step toward the strange lady.

"Yep. And Duncan and if I am right, Glenna too. Though I guess this is her past so she might not know me yet. This is so nuts."

"Nuts. What have nuts got to do with it?"

Molly walked towards them.

"I am not aware of who you are." It was true. She had never seen this woman before but her being on the hill made it possible that she was on the hill from the future.

What were the fae up to?

Molly stopped in her tracks. "Whoa...I feel dizzy. Rachael said I might feel strange. She was right."

She started to slump toward the ground but before she reached it Alasdair caught the black-haired maiden and swooped her into his arms.

"She has fainted. Just like Rachael did when she came from the future. Let us take her home." And he started heading down the path of the hill. He carried the lass as if she weighted nothing.

What was going on?

Glenna looked around her. No sign of teal blue light or figures anywhere.

"What are you fae up to?" she asked the empty space around her.

Molly kept her eyes closed. She listened. Birds tweeting. Insects buzzing. The occasional sound of horse's hooves on the gravel outside. She knew she was inside as she was enjoying the comfort of a bed beneath her. She had made it. She was in the past. Unless she was on her bed at Mrs Watson's. But no. The sound of horse's hooves dispensed with that theory. She opened her eyes slowly.

In front of her was a window, curtained in green velvet and in front of the window sat Glenna reading a book. Then she remembered. She was lightheaded. She must have passed out. They, Glenna, and the man she assumed was Glenna's brother, Alasdair must have brought her back to the castle.

"I see you have woken."

Molly pulled herself into a sitting position. Glenna got up and went to the door. She pulled on what looked like a bellpull. Would that really summon servants?

"Yes. It is so good to see you, Glenna."

"Do I know you?"

"Well...yes. In the future. You and Rachael spent some time with me discussing...er well many things."

"I see. That is strange as I have no intention of going to the future."

"I know, but you will." She lifted her hand to her head. "It really can give you a headache thinking about it, doesn't it? This time travel stuff."

"I would not know as I have not travelled through time."

"Then you believe me?"

"I do, but because of what you are wearing, and your accent is similar to Rachael's. And because I know the fae are behind this."

"I know. I was so excited when I met Rachael. I'm Australian too."

"Yes, I had assumed as much. But why are you here?"

"That is a long story. Can I share it with you and Alasdair together, please?"

"Of course." She came back and sat in the chair as the door opened.

A big brass bathtub was brought in by two burly looking gentlemen dressed in black. A maid dashed forward and laid a thick blanket on the floor. The men placed the bathtub down on the blanket and left. A string of girls—maids—came in and placed hot water into the bathtub. Bucket full after bucket full. She could see the steam rise as the level in the bath rose.

"We will give you time to freshen up. You have slept for some hours. There will be a maid outside this door. I have brought you a dress to wear. We appear to be similar sizes." Glenna indicated the dress draped over the chair. It was a beautiful forest green. She loved the colour.

"The maid will bring you down to the library when you are ready. We can have tea. I will have some food for you to eat also."

"Thank you, Glenna, I won't be long."

"Take your time, Molly. You have plenty of it." She curtsied and turned and left the room.

Glenna closed the door behind her and indicated to the maid, Lizzie, to wait at the closed door. This was not like when Rachael had arrived. This woman knew she had come back in time and needed no convincing, unlike when Rachael had arrived. They too knew she was from the future and so did not have to treat her like a spy. The king had been and gone again.

Did this Molly really know her? Molly accepted her without

question. That was also strange. And Alasdair had carried her all the way back to the castle, with a smile upon his face. He too had accepted that she was from the future where they knew their brother and Rachael had gone.

She made her way down to the library and found her brother sitting and awaiting her arrival.

"I take it Molly has woken?"

"Yes, and she is now bathing and will join us in the not-too-distant future." She chuckled at herself as she made her way to the settee.

"She is telling the truth." It was a statement of fact, not a question. Her brother needed no convincing as to where she had come from.

"She would appear to be. She wants to tell us all about why she has come when we are together. She wants us to know as much as possible."

"Do you believe her?"

"Yes brother. She is aware of her being in the past. Her face lights up at anything strange to her. Just as Rachael's did when she came. I have no doubt. But I have many questions as to why she has come and her telling us she knows me. I have no intention to go to the future. It is so strange."

"Do you want to go to the future?"

"No more than you. I just want to know Duncan and Rachael are safe. But I have no plans to go and find out what the future holds."

"I then suggest we wait to hear what Molly has to say and discover why she has come."

"Yes. I am sure she will tell us all." She looked at Dair. He was accepting. Last time he had doubted everything, but he had changed. He had become a believer. She, however, was wondering what the fae were doing.

Soaking in the water and the atmosphere of the castle she knew in the future, was a relaxing pastime. She breathed in the fragrance of the lavender soap they had given to her to wash herself with. This whole experience was very civilised. She had not been sure what to expect. After all history had played very little in her past life. But now...

The maid helped her to dress and that was strange too. As was the lack of underwear. The maid, Lizzie, also helped her get her hair in order. Not just tied back but curled and pinned in the style of the early 1800's. She would ask Glenna to confirm what year it was. For her own benefit. She was not the historian Rachael was. She just wanted to get the feel of this new old castle and the time she was in. Finally, she was ready and headed downstairs.

At the bottom of the stairs one of the footmen waited to escort her to the library. The maid, Lizzie, curtsied and headed back upstairs. She pulled the neckline up as this dress was very feminine. Strange clothes for a chef who usually wandered around in loose trousers and a chef's jacket. The slippers were a perfect size. Rachael had told her they were not called shoes. Learning all these different names and ways to live could be an exciting pastime.

The footman opened the door to the library and announced her.

"Miss Molly."

She stepped into the room as Glenna and the man stood.

"Molly Grace. My name is Molly Grace." But in her head the nursery rhyme was singing. *Miss Molly had a dolly who was sick, sick, sick.* She could hear her mother's voice in her head.

She came over to Alasdair and took his hand and shook it.

He did not let go and stared into her eyes.

"You must be Alasdair."

"I am."

He paused but still did not let go of her hand. "I must say that Glenna's dress looks very becoming on you."

"Thank you. You are the sweet talker Rachael said you would be." She pulled her hand out of his and went to stand next to Glenna.

His politeness disappeared. He became serious.

Opps, she might have offended him.

"Well, I suggest we sit down, and you explain to us how you know Rachael and my brother."

Sigh. Maybe she had said the wrong thing.

"Come and sit with me." Glenna indicated the settee where she could sit.

The servants came and placed the tea on a table nearby and served tea to all three of them. She was offered a cup and then had both sugar and milk in front of her.

"Thank you but I take mine black with none."

She could sense Alasdair's eyes wandering all over her. He was trying to make her out. She understood. A strange woman, with a strange accent, showing up out of nowhere. She planned to watch him too. Especially at his reactions as she told her story. She had no concern for Glenna, she would believe, but him?

She took a sip of her tea and began...

4

BACK IN ABERLOUR

Scotland, 2020

Molly dried herself and got into a clean pair of jeans, but instead of a T-shirt she put on a beautiful blue floral shirt that her mum had sent her for Christmas. Molly could feel her mum every time she put it on. It was like she was being hugged. She missed her mum and could not believe that she too had gone and left her all alone. She sat at the desk and looked at the framed photo of her.

Wanting to go home after the death of her sister and niece, she had called her mum. Rumours were already racing around the world about a virus. Mum wanted her to stay in Edinburgh and to keep working. They had agreed that her mum would come and visit her and maybe even stay until this bug was gone. But she had a cruise to go on first. And Mr. Right could be on the cruise. A cruise she had saved up for, for years. One that would be the death of her.

Molly and her mum, Carina, would talk for hours. A memory

she would hold close to her heart. The tears began to fall again. Her mum was beautiful, even at fifty-five, there was no doubting her beauty. Her black hair, with the odd strand of grey, long and surrounding her smiling face. She had her mother's hair. Her mum's smile would capture all around her. As would her sky-blue eyes. She had her mum's eyes too. She absorbed all in the photo. It had been taken at Christmas just gone before the deaths of Skye and Flora. Her father, Sen, had walked out on them when she was only three and Skye was five. She never heard from him again. And right now, she had no desire to see him even though she was alone. She had no memory of him. Sen Kalen, a Scot, who she knew nothing about.

There was a knock at the door.

"Come in, aunty." Molly called.

"Molly dear. Come and have some more tea. I have two friends I would like you to meet."

"No problem, aunty. I will be right down."

Mrs Watson closed the door.

Molly cleaned her nose and dried the last of her tears. She grabbed a few more tissues and stuck them in her pocket. She brushed her hair then she went downstairs.

Mrs Watson had not had any visitors since she came to stay. COVID-19 had seen to that. She had come for a week's stay at Aberlour. She had picked the village as she wanted to try the whisky, famous from here. 'Aberlour', the sixteen-year-old was quite a treat. Then lockdown hit.

She came into the lounge and two young ladies stood as she entered. They were wearing face masks as she was. Meeting people was so strange. You saw their eyes but really nothing else. Were they smiling? She could not tell even if she wanted to. But there was a sense that pervaded the room. Friendship. That could be down to it being Mrs Watson's home. But it felt good.

"Molly Grace, I am so delighted to meet you. I am Rachael Murray, and this is my sister-in-law, Glenna."

Molly came over and was about the shake their hand when she said, "Sorry, force of habit." She gave them a gentle wave.

"Would you mind if I take off the mask? I would like you to see our faces. And we can keep the required distance from each other."

"It's okay by me."

Everyone slipped off their masks.

Mrs. Watson went over to the window and opened it. "Just to let the air move around you girls."

Rachael was smiling sweetly at her, but Glenna had a look of shock on her face. But she could not determine why. Glenna looked at Rachael and then back at her.

"Now, sit down girls and get to know each other while I get the pot of tea." Mrs. Watson retreated to the kitchen.

"Murray. Are you from the manor?"

"Sort of. We live in the stone house on the edge of the estate. I am married to Duncan Murray."

"Oh, I think I know him. I saw him driving around in that big black Land Rover. He is very tall, isn't he?"

"Yes, that's him. Yes, he's tall and he loves that black beast."

"You must love living in this neck of the woods. But do I detect an Aussie accent?"

"Yes, you do. I came from Dubbo in NSW. Where are you from?"

"Melbourne."

"I bet you are glad not to be there at the moment?"

"Yes and no."

"Aunty Jess has told us about your family. Your sister and niece died in a car accident—I believe?"

"Yes unfortunately." Molly lowered her head and looked at her feet. But she held the tears at bay. She took in a deep breath.

"And your mum from COVID?"

"Yep. She was on the Ruby Princess when it docked in Sydney." She took another deep breath.

"Oh dear. There were a lot of people who died on that ship. I am sorry."

"So am I. She was too young. Only fifty-five. She had no underlying health issues either. She was in the wrong place at the wrong time."

"I do understand. And I am so sorry. That was all your family, wasn't it?"

"Yep. I have a dad out there somewhere, but he hasn't been in touch since he left us when I was a little kid. I don't have any real memory of him. Skye could remember him but only just."

"I am so sorry to bring bad memories back to you."

"Hey, it isn't your fault. This is my life now. But thank you for your concern."

"I know I must sound like a nosy neighbour, but I have been concerned for you. It is such a bad time. And I wanted you to know that you are not alone."

"That is nice of you but why?"

"I lost my mum and dad in a car accident some years ago. I came here to help heal my own heart. I just would like the same thing for you."

"I am sorry. Did you have any siblings?"

"No. I was truly alone, so I understand a bit what you must be feeling like and going through."

"Gee thanks, Rachael." She could feel a tear make its way down her cheek. She wiped it away.

"So, in part I am here so you can share your story. To know someone is listening. Aunty Jess did that for me too when I came." Rachael added.

"What, were you staying here? That is incredible. I have to ask...did you find healing on the Fairy Hill, behind the town?"

"Actually, I did in many ways."

"Did you find your handsome husband on the hill? Sorry but he is handsome."

"Don't apologise. He is handsome. I get it."

Glenna stood and walked around the room. She would stop and look at Molly and then start walking again.

"I am sorry to single your brother out like that." Molly directed her comment to Glenna. Maybe by involving her, it might help her to settle. It was like she was walking around on hot rocks.

"That is perfectly acceptable." She replied in her very best English. "I am just surprised you had time to notice."

"A handsome man walks by, I notice. I might not do anything, but I notice. It reminds me that I am still alive." She looked back at Rachael who was grinning and nodding. "Hope you don't mind?"

"Not at all. And he has brothers."

Molly laughed out loud. "Oh, I want to meet them." And deep in her heart she did. She had not laughed out loud for so long. She smiled at Rachael.

Mrs Watson came back in and poured the tea for everyone.

"I have been open with Molly. I have told her about the fairies and the Fairy Hill. She is questioning things. Perhaps she could do with a change of scene." She put the teapot down, her questioning gaze settling on Rachael.

"Aunty Jess believes you might be open to the belief in the fae?"

"I must admit strange things have happened on that hill. It seems to have a life all its own. Distant and cut off from the rest of the world. But fairies?"

"Do you think you could believe?"

"I am open to hear what you have to say. I might add, I would like some proof if there were anything."

"May I tell you a story? It might help you to believe. If you will allow me?"

"Sure. Give it your best shot. I have nothing to lose." A tear slowly flowed down her cheek. She wiped it away.

Glenna came over and took Molly's hand. In her light Scottish accent, with less of the English formality, she added,

"Your heart will heal."

Over the next three hours Rachael shared her story. Coming to Scotland, dreaming of her man in the painting. Her time here but in the past. Falling for Duncan. Believing he was lost to her. All of it. Even her pregnancy which Molly could now notice.

"Well Duncan's brother has to wear some of the blame."

"He did." Glenna added. "It took him a long time to come to terms with what he did. He thought he was being punished, then...he believes now about the fae and how Rachael and Duncan needed to be together."

Molly nodded. "Well, I must say all of this information has given me a great deal to think about."

Rachael stood and took Molly into her arms.

"I know we are not supposed to hug but I need you to know I care."

Molly hugged her back. "Thank you. I do appreciate it. Being alone for a while now, I crave hugs. Bloody COVID."

Rachael let go. "There is more I wish to talk to you about. I would like for you to come for dinner, meet Duncan and some of the other family at the castle. I have a proposition for you."

5

BUIN CASTLE

1823

Glenna's eyes were wide open as she listened intently to her story. She was excited but Alasdair's demeanour concerned her. Though definitely paying attention to the story, he showed concern, even fear as he listened to every word. Sweat gathered on his forehead, showing her the fear surrounding him. He then got up and started pacing the room.

"I haven't finished my story, but I see you want to ask questions. This has been more intense than I thought. So why don't we stop, and you can ask some questions and hopefully we can move on. Are you okay, Alasdair? I am sorry if I have said anything that hurts you."

"Please. If you don't mind, how is Rachael?" He didn't smile but seemed tense, waiting for the reply.

"She is glowing. When I first met her, she was about six months gone. But when I left..."

"She is with child still?" Alasdair asked. His expression was one of concern.

"She was. She had a baby girl just before I came here. They call her Clara Jean Murray."

She watched him sit down again. A load had been taken off his shoulders. She almost felt his breath leave his body as the relief took hold of him.

"Clara Jean. Clara. I like it. Thank you for giving me this news. The birth of a child does not always go well. It is wonderful to know they are now a family."

"Molly, it is good to know that Rachael and Duncan have a family. These are questions that have been running around in our heads. Not knowing if they are happy or what kind of future, they will have..."

"I understand, for the future is a confusing place for me to be in. I can imagine how you both must think about it. I have no one of my family left. That is in part why I decided to see what the past might hold." She lowered her head. "I have lost everything."

"Please Molly, I would like to take you on a walk around the grounds. Let you see the castle as it is now. I think a break from all this future knowledge will do us all the world of good. Some fresh air. Do you not agree?"

"Thank you, Alasdair, I think I would like that. I must admit I am tired."

Alasdair stood and offered her his arm. She stood and placed her arm around his. He smiled and they left the library. Suddenly things were different. And she hadn't finished telling her story. Now she was asking herself, why was she here?Does the past offer her anything of value? And here is a brother of Duncan. A very handsome one.

"I must apologise for stopping you telling more of your story. It has been a great deal of a shock."

"A shock? But you knew they had gone to be together?"

He glanced at the beauty walking next to him. She could not guess the pain that permeated him. The pain he had inflicted on his brother and Rachael. He knew she had laid the blame at his feet. He knew he deserved being condemned but by this lass who did not know him. It was disturbing.

"Yes, you are right. But your arrival too. I cannot see into the future. I have wondered if they are happy and if they will live a long and happy life. It pains me not to know. The fact you have seen them recently just adds to the confusion of the future. Did we make the right decisions?"

"I can imagine my coming would shock you." She paused. He looked at her. "Are you still in love with Rachael?"

He lowered his head again and watched his feet as they walked slowly over the green grass in front of the castle. She knew him perhaps better than he thought.

"I do not love Rachael. Perhaps I thought I did for a while. I will admit I lusted after her. You must think me a villain. But it was wrong. I know that now. I wanted what my brother wanted, and he wanted Rachael with all his heart. But I cannot tell my brother I am sorry. I tried before he left but I am not sure he believed me or forgave me."

She was silent for a moment. He was watching her silently, perhaps hoping she would hear the truth in his words. She looked back at him. Their eyes fixed on each other, and they stopped to deepen the gaze. He wondered if they were looking into each other's souls.

"I am no expert in this time travel stuff, but I know you have been keeping diaries. Am I right?"

He dropped his gaze to his feet. "Yes…but what has that got to do with my not being able to talk to him."

"Write to your brother. Tell him of your pain. Tell him you only want them to be happy. I know he will read all your diaries for the rest of your life." She shook her head. "Write what is in your heart. He will read your thoughts. He will know, eventually, if he doesn't already."

He lifted his eyes to again investigate the pools of bright blue that were her own.

He lifted her hand to his lips and kissed her fingers.

"Thank you, Molly. You are right. Your thoughts have given me hope. Thank you. Can I show you the stables?"

Boy, he took her breath away. His hair was ruffled and reddish brown. He wasn't the carrot red which was a Scottish trademark. It was lighter and had a good dash of brown in it. He was handsome, she could not deny it but a bit of a lady killer from all she had heard. But here he was concerned for his brother and sister-in-law. His heart was aching. She could see it on his face. And then he kissed her hand, and her stomach did a somersault. He was not making a move on her. He was sincerely grateful for the knowledge she shared with him. That was the only reason he kissed her fingers. Gratitude.

This is not the image of the Alasdair she had conjured up before she had arrived. He had changed. He was different. Rachael had not seen the change that had occurred in him, after his rash actions. The loss of his brother had changed the way he thought.

The way he felt. The way he behaved. He was sullen, quiet even melancholy. He wanted them to be happy and because he did not know if they were, he had been punishing himself. Severely.

Walking with him gave her time to re-evaluate the conclusions she had made of him. She listened when he spoke. Detected his pride in his family, in what they have achieved. His love of the countryside around him. Their estate and most important his love for his brother Duncan. It was good, she had paid him attention. She took in deep breathes and noted the faint smells of grass, hay, and horses. She heard the insects buzzing and plopping. It was like a symphony of nature's sounds. After going the long way around, they finally arrived at the stables.

As they entered, she detected a lift in his spirits.

"I love to ride. Meet 'Black Robbie'. He was Duncan's horse. But now he is mine. I am so happy to be looking after him. He is a fine figure of a horse. I just call him 'Robbie'. Do you ride?" He was animated.

"Actually, I have never ridden a horse. In the future...but I would love to learn." She looked into his eyes. "Would you be willing to teach me? Not on Black Robbie though." She gave a tentative smile.

"Are you planning to stay?"

"Well...I am hoping you will let me. I need to fill you in with what else we talked about, in the future, I mean..."

"I am happy for you to stay, for a while. I do want to hear more of Duncan and Rachael, and life for them. But I also want to know more of your story."

Sudden heat rose to her neck. "Shall we go back into the castle and join Glenna and I can continue where I left off."

"Yes, let us. But take your time. We can discuss all your story, as you have all the time in the world. And you do, have as much time as you like. I would like you to stay as long as you want to. I know what it is to lose family you love. Perhaps we can help each other?"

Heat flooded her cheeks. "Perhaps."

"I do not want to embarrass you. I only want you to enjoy your stay. I would like us to be friends."

"I would like that too. Thank you."

He offered his arm to her and carefully looped her arm through his. A rush of happiness went through her as she held on to him and saw his smile.

They made their way back to the castle. The weather was changing. It was cooler as the sun was setting in the west. But the colours of deep blue and grey with just a touch of pink, took her breath away. Already this countryside was healing her soul. She was glad to be here. In the past. Holding on to this man.

"Come Molly and freshen up." Glenna turned to her brother. "We will dress for dinner and see you in the dining room in an hour."

"Very well, in an hour. I will tell cook." Alasdair bowed and then addressed Molly. "We can continue your story then if you wish. But remember you have all the time in the world."

"Thank you. I will keep your words in mind."

And he turned and headed for the kitchen.

"My brother has brightened since you began to tell your story. He was anxious but you seem to have calmed him."

"I must admit I am glad to see I have brought both of you comfort, with the knowledge of your brother and Rachael and the baby. I don't think they realised how important it was for you both to hear what they have done since they returned to the future."

They both turned and made their way upstairs.

"Come with me and you can look at my gowns. You are a perfect fit in my clothes, and you may choose a few gowns to wear. We can also look at what Rachael had and have any you like, altered."

"That would be delightful. Can we not say any more about my story until we return to your brother?"

"But of course." They continued up the stairs. "What is concerning you, Molly?"

Molly looked at Glenna.

"Not a concern but I do want to make sure I cover everything. It is tiring work to go through all the details. I don't want to miss anything, and I want to be sure you both get the information you need. I saw the relief in your brother's eyes as he heard how happy Rachael and Duncan are."

"You are doing Rachael and Duncan proud. And I do not deny the relief for both of us to know the future is bright for them. Thank you, Molly." They entered Glenna's room.

"Is this your room?"

"It is, why? You seemed surprised."

"This is the room I stayed in before I came back in time. No wonder I felt at home when I visited the castle." She looked around the room. "It is the same but different. That beautiful four-poster bed is still there."

She took a seat near the fireplace and closed her eyes. The image of the future room was there in her head.

"This is so weird."

"You really do sound like Rachael."

She opened her eyes and looked at Glenna. "That is a great

compliment. Thank you, Glenna. I feel like I am learning all about you all over again."

"As you said, it is weird."

They smiled at each other. Suddenly Molly knew she had not only found a friend in Glenna, again, but she knew she had made the right decision to come back in time. She would try to relax and enjoy the experience.

6

THE FOOD

1823

As Molly entered the dining room with Glenna, he was again taken aback by the future lady's beauty. His intake of breath even surprised him. She had changed her dress to a dark blue silk, that matched her eyes, making them shine all the brighter. He was looking forward to hearing more of her story, and of her experiences with Duncan and Rachael. He kept his eyes upon her as she came toward the table.

He stood to greet them as they took their seats.

"You both look beautiful." He watched the blush take hold of Molly's angelic face. His sister smiled at him. She had seen he had meant the compliment for Molly. He returned the grin.

They sat and the servants placed the first course of dinner in front of each of them, a potato soup.

Molly stared at it and took some deep breathes, closing her eyes as she did so.

"It smells heavenly. Is it potato?"

"It is. Ah yes you are a cook in the future. I mean chef. A most unusual profession for a woman like yourself."

"Not really. I love cooking. Perhaps later, another day, I can prepare some of my favourite meals for you. After all I did work in one of the best restaurants in Edinburgh."

He heard the pride in her voice. She loved her previous employment; he could see it on her face.

"Restaurant. That's French, is it not?"

"Yes. Food that restores. But in my time, it is a place to eat when you don't want to cook, or you want to meet with friends. Most of us don't have our own cooks at home. My mother loved to cook, so that is where I got my love of cooking, I guess."

"I am sure you did. If it will please you, you could perhaps teach our cook some of the meals you once prepared. But only if you wish. This is a time for you to relax, remember?"

"Yes. I do understand. But I would like to. I have done little cooking since I left Edinburgh, and I would love to see some of the recipes your cook uses."

She lifted the soup spoon and tried it. She closed her eyes, and an expression of total enjoyment took over her features. He thought it strange. Rachael closed her eyes to remember. But Molly closed her eyes to create the memory.

She sighed. "That is the most glorious soup I think I have ever tasted."

"Very high compliments for cook. She will love meeting you."

"I agree." Added Glenna. "Mrs. Gillies will adore you if you continue to talk of her food with such excitement."

"Oh, I mean it." She licked the spoon clean and dipped it into the soup again.

No one said another word until Molly had finished her bowl, just ahead of him.

The butler cleared the plates.

"I want the recipe. Glorious."

"Did you want to share any more information? About the future?"

"Yes. In fact, I left off when Rachael wanted me to have dinner at the castle and meet some of the family. You see meals are very important to me."

B*uin Castle, 2020*

It was two days since she had spent time with Rachael and Glenna. She was looking forward to having dinner with them, other family members and meeting Duncan. She had worn her coat over her dress. Yes, a dress. A pretty blue, tight fitting with an A-line skirt. She very rarely went out in a dress. In fact, she only had one with her. It was suitable for dinner and a show, so it would be suitable for the manor house/castle. She wore flats, as she often did. That was more suitable anyway as she had decided to walk to the castle.

She went up the stairs and knocked on the door. It was still light as the butler opened the door and ushered her inside.

Rachael came toward her and greeted her with a hug.

"I know we are not supposed to hug, but I can't help myself. I find it a hard habit to break."

"I think we can forgive each other this minor hiccup."

"I am so glad you are here. I want you to meet Duncan."

The tall man she had seen many times in the village stepped forward.

"Greetings Molly. Let me take your coat." And he helped her take it off. "Racheal has spoken very highly of you. I am looking forward to spending time with you and getting to know you as she has done."

"Thank you, Duncan. I feel I know you already. Thank you for allowing me to see inside this beautiful castle."

"It is our pleasure. Now come with me and let me introduce you to the laird and to some of the other family members."

They made their way down a beautifully furnished hallway to the dining room where many other people were gathered. The room was also decorated immaculately. All stood as she entered the room.

A sudden heat flushed through to her face. She was probably bright red. She had to admit being the centre of attention was something she would never get used to. Duncan pulled a chair out for her to sit in then another for Rachael. Glenna came to the other side of the table and sat opposite her.

"This is a beautiful room."

"It is and just the way it was when I was here so long ago. It has modern features also, but this is the table my parents bought."

She touched the wood of the table and wondered how many people had sat here and had meals over the many years. She adored the way Duncan spoke freely of his being from the past around her. Oh, he made her honoured and trusted in a way she was never before. She was swelling with pride, and she sat straight in the chair.

Duncan stood and introduced the family members. The current laird, also Duncan by name and his wife, Dianna. Both greeted her with a smile. A beautiful young lady who looked like Glenna, Anna, sat there with her new husband, Henry Peters, a doctor. The laird's sister, Jocelyn, was also there, mother to Anna. Jocelyn's husband had recently passed away from COVID.

"He had some other medical issues that weakened him. He was in hospital when the virus infected several staff. Unfortunately, he did not have the strength to fight it." Jocelyn's face was sad and tired.

"We hope he didn't suffer." Added Anna, a tear rolling down her cheek.

"I am so sorry to hear of your loss. My mother was on the Ruby Princess when it docked in Sydney. She too became sick. But she was very healthy. It is terrible what this virus can do and who it will affect. You can be sick or very healthy. There is no rhyme or reason as to who gets it or dies."

A tear rolled down her own cheek.

"No more sadness, please. We are one big happy family together now and Molly, we are glad that you have joined us." Rachael stood. "I propose a toast." Rachael lifted her orange juice as others lifted their wine or champagne.

"To Molly and all the family who believe."

"To Molly." The sound echoed around the room.

She stood, "To all."

"To all." came the echo.

The dinner was wonderful, and they all spoke of so many things but especially of the way in which the family had experienced the fae. The history of Fairy Hill was fascinating. She learned the fae had been part of that site for thousands of years and through many generations of the Murray family.

"In some respects," added Rachael, "It's as if anyone with fairy blood or a belief in them seem to be attracted to the site."

She had not spoken much during the evening but had concentrated on listening to all the information. All of it was overwhelming and fascinating at the same time. But Rachael's comment stirred something within her.

"When I first went up onto the hill, I was drawn to it. In fact, I fell asleep the first time I was there and have on other subsequent visits. It has helped me to heal, I believe. After I have slept, I am refreshed. That is why I believe in the fae. They have reached out and touched me. I have never thought about fae or magic before. In Australia it is not fae legends we think about. Aboriginal magic and beliefs are so different. With what has happened to me, I can't deny their existence in the here and now. I am a believer, I guess."

"It is still a monumental step in faith you have taken. There would be others who would argue you were going crazy."

"I know. I think I thought I was. But I always felt better after a night slept on the hill. And Mrs. Watson thought me normal. She said I needed to heal. Needed the hill to heal me. And that made sense to me."

"And I think she was right." Anna looked directly into her eyes. "The hill needs you. Do you think you can take the next step?"

"This is weird. I think I know what the next step is, even though you have not spoken about it." Molly paused, looking at the faces of all the people sitting around her.

"What do you think the next step is?" Anna never took her eyes from Molly.

"To allow the fae to take me to the past."

She watched the family look at each other. Some surprised, others smiling.

"Yes, Molly. I think this is a chance for you to fulfil your destiny."

"Destiny." She repeated the word and a strange feeling of happiness filled her. Through the months of pain, the words filled her with a joy and peace she had not felt for a long time. "Destiny."

Rachael took her hand.

"I think Anna might be right. This is the proposition I was

going to make. Spend some time in the past to renew yourself and heal from the sadness. What do you think?"

"I want to go. I want to go to the past. I can't explain it."

Glenna looked into her eyes from across the dining table.

"I sense the fae in you. There must be a reason you need to go back. We will help you achieve your goal. Don't be afraid."

"The fae in me..." She said no more but her mind began to imagine what the fae were like and if she resembled them in any way. Either in thought or in appearance.

Why would she think like that?

7
DESTINY

1823

"This is remarkable." He knew he sounded excited. But he did not want to hide it.

"Not really. I just felt I needed to come."

"But you believe. And so quickly. It took me years to accept the fae were part of our family."

"I guess I was pushed closer to belief due to my circumstances."

"You mean your losses." he whispered.

"Yes, I guess so." She lowered her head. "I was needing something. But I was drawn to the hill. That was very real to me. I really did feel refreshed when I came down each time, after I had fallen asleep."

"I understand. Since Duncan left, we have walked to the hill nearly every day. It brings Glenna and I closer to Duncan and Rachael. We know they will not be coming back but I really feel close to them when I sit there."

"That is the strangest part. I did not feel it bring me closer to my family. I was just relieved of some of the loss, the pain of not having them anymore. I know they are gone, and I will never see them again. There are no promises of a reunion just a relief."

"Whereas I know my brother is alive and well, in the future. Is that what you mean?" He frowned and lowered his gaze.

"I'm sorry. I don't mean to sound critical. But yes, you know he has a future. A future you might not see or know about. Or even be a part of. My family have none now, never to return. I don't even know what I want to do, now I am without them."

"I think I understand. I am sorry."

"Please don't apologise. Your pain and loss are just as great. Don't get me wrong. It's just different."

He looked at her across the table. Her pain was different. He knew the loss of parents. But not a sibling or of an innocent. After all, she was right, Duncan was still alive and well in the future, even if he had difficulty understanding how it could be. Yet he still believed it.

She smiled and he did his best to smile back. But he was disappointed with himself. This was not about him. It was about her. Her healing. He needed to remember her. He wanted to change the discussion. Move on.

"What of the main course. Was it to your satisfaction?"

She laughed. "Thank you, Alasdair, it was beautiful. Venison is such a beautiful piece of meat. And the sauce your cook used was delectable."

"Then let us continue your story while we wait for dessert."

She smiled and then looked at Glenna.

Glenna took her hand. "You are a remarkable woman, Molly."

Molly laughed out loud. "That's what you told me in the future. My head hurts again."

They all laughed. After a moment she continued.

"So, after dinner..."

2020

Sitting in the library surrounded by Murrays was a wonderful experience. Each one was welcoming, and it was as if she knew them all intimately. They were family. That's what it was like. She shook her head internally. They were not her family, but she loved the fact they treated her as if she was a member of theirs.

"So, you want to go back?" Duncan asked the question she was not sure she could answer again but she gave it a try.

"I think so. Everything points to it. The fact I could feel it here inside my heart," she placed her hand over her heart, "I need to see what the past might hold for me."

"Then if you are determined, we will help you. Sam, do you have your pad of paper with you?"

"Sure do."

Sam was Rachael's best friend. She had come to the Murrays estate to organise the historical documents and maintain their library. She also worked for Rachael parttime so that Rachael could write. Sam was a bundle of energy. Another person she was glad to get to know.

"Then let us work out what we need to prepare."

"Will there be much to prepare?" She looked around at all the smiling faces.

"A few things. You can't take anything with you, like a bag. Only what is on your person at the time." Rachael added.

"Okay...but I think I want to wait till you have had your baby."

Rachael looked bewildered. "Why?"

"I think Glenna and Alasdair will want to know that you are safe and so is the child. I can take a photo or two with me."

"She's right." Glenna jumped in. "Now my head hurts. But it is true. As you are expecting, then it would be so much better to know you and the babe are safe."

"Besides, I want to go into seclusion after we have arranged everything. I do not want to take COVID with me to the past. It would be irresponsible. And they could not handle it."

"That is commendable, and I will help you. I will arrange for you to have your vaccine as soon as possible." Added Dr Peters.

"Besides, we want you to know some things about our plans, the plans we made with Alasdair, so he knows what will work and what will not. It's funny though, all the things we planned, the whisky, the shortbread, the tourists have worked out very well. The Murray clan have a wonderful future ahead of them both then and now."

"I think it would also be better for you to move into the big house."

"Thank you, Dianna, but can I wait a few more weeks before I do? I need to prepare some things. I might return from the past and I might not. I am very aware you probably already know if I do, or I don't. But I still need to do certain things. Just in case I stay longer than I anticipate."

1823

"What things did you have to prepare?"

"Lots. I will reveal what I did over time. You see I don't know if I am staying in the past yet."

"I understand." He lowered his head and took a deep breath. She was watching the pain she had, seeping into him. He wanted to share it with her. Bear her burden. That is what she sensed in him.

"The most important thing was for me to finalise my mother's estate and sell the family home. My sister's estate had almost been completed. She didn't have a lot. But I had to make sure they were sorted before I left. Phone calls, emails and Zoom meetings with the lawyers back in Australia helped me get things moving. The money I had I wanted to be used for the Murray estate if I don't go back. So, I arranged things with Duncan. Powers of attorney, if I did not come back. Things like that. And then I had to work out what I would bring with me."

"May I ask what you brought, Molly?"

"Yes Glenna." She looked at her hand. "My mother's ring. A light blue square sapphire surrounded by diamonds." She lifted her hand and showed them both the ring. The stone, she knew, also had matched her mother's light blue eyes.

"It is beautiful."

"It reminds me of her, every day. My mother was Carina Grace. And I am proud of her." She lowered her hand and fiddled with her ring. After a moment she went on. "This necklace." She lifted her hand to the line of silver chain around her neck. "It is a pearl set with diamonds. It belonged to my sister Skye. She never had anything fancy, but she cherished this. Mum had given it to her when she graduated as a nurse. Mum sent it to me after she died. This simple design reminds me of her."

"And what of your niece, Flora?" Alasdair asked.

She lifted her gaze to his chiselled features. Pain was still there. He was winning her over with his care and thoughtfulness. He was truly interested in her reply. He seemed so unlike the man she had imagined.

"Flora made a band of coloured cottons that she twisted into a bracelet. For a sweet three-year-old she did a lovely job. She gave it to me at Christmas." She lifted her other hand to show them. "I will wear it on special occasions. It is very fragile. Just as Flora was."

"Did you bring anything else?"

"Yes, Glenna. I needed to convince you both, Rachael and Duncan would be okay. I believe from my discussions with Glenna in the future that Rachael told you both about photography."

"Yes, she did. A remarkable piece of future science." His expression brightened.

"Is that what you have brought? A photo?" Glenna asked.

Molly looked around at the servants. She was unsure who knew what. But Alasdair could read her mind it would seem. He dismissed the footmen and asked them to bring tea to the library in fifteen minutes. Then he stood and came to sit next to Molly. He took her hand.

"We await your reveal."

"I didn't know these beautiful dresses had hidden pockets until Glenna showed me earlier. I was worried how I could hide them." She reached her other hand into the hidden side pocket and pulled out three photos.

The first was a wedding photo of Rachael and Duncan. The second was of them holding their beautiful daughter between them on a lounge. The third was of the three of them standing outside their lodge.

She handed them to Alasdair.

He reverently took them and examined each one quietly. He made no comment. Then handed them to Glenna who in turn handled them with great reverence.

"They are for you to do with as you see fit. I know that they are not of this time, and you will not want them on display but yes they are for you."

"Thank you." He whispered. "Thank you with all my heart."

"Yes, thank you." Added Glenna.

"You are both welcome. I hope they bring you joy."

Alasdair stood and offered his arm to Molly who graciously accepted it.

"Now let us have tea." He added and they headed for the library.

8

NOW WHAT?

1823

She laid in the bed, warm and content. Watching the faces of those from the past seeing photos for the first time, was a magical moment. It had put a smile on her face she still could not get rid of. It was good she had brought them. Along with a few hundred tablets of Ibuprofen. They might come in handy and be helpful.

She took a deep breath in and could detect the fragrance of lavender. Was she still smelling the soap she used when she had her bath the previous afternoon? She buried her head into the pillow. The fragrance was there. It was all around her. Tears welled in her eyes. She had remembered when she had bathed that her mother loved lavender. But it had not stirred the emotions building in her now. She sat up and leaned back into the pillows behind her.

The fragrance was wafting through the room, but she could not determine where it was coming from. Perhaps the maid had placed a vase of lavender in the room that she had not seen.

Mum.

There was a knock at the door and a maid came in and went to the window and opened the curtains. Light flooded the bedroom.

"Excuse me, miss. Miss Glenna thought you might like to start the day with a cup of tea as Miss Rachael did." She blushed and returned to the door.

"Hello and yes I would like a cuppa. And your name is?"

"Morag, miss. I was maid to Miss Rachael before..."

The girl's face dropped its smile. Suddenly she was sad. She curtsied and left the room. Perhaps she didn't know they were safe in the future. She was sure to ask Glenna.

A footman came in with a tray that held a tea pot and two cups. He placed the tray on the table and left, just as Glenna entered.

"You do like to drink tea, do you not?"

"You bet. us Aussies love a good cuppa. Some love coffee but it is tea for me."

Glenna grinned and came to the table and poured the cups.

"Put your dressing gown on and come and sit down."

"Okay, I will. This bed is so comfortable." She got up, placed the gown around her shoulders and came to the table and sat in the chair. She looked around the room trying to determine where the lavender was coming from.

"Is something amiss? I can see you have been crying." Glenna asked also looking around the room.

"No. Just memories. Even here in the past I cannot escape those who have gone. My mother loved lavender and the fragrance is so strong here."

Glenna came to the bed and pointed up at the two posts at the end of the four-poster.

"The maids occasionally attach fresh lavender to make the room smell sweet and clean."

Molly came over and looked up to the top of the post and saw a small bundle of lavender flowers tied with a ribbon to the post near the curtains that hung from the bed. She smiled.

"Would you like them removed?"

"No. On the contrary. It made me think of my mother. Thank you for explaining. I like the idea. Makes Mum feel close to me, even here in the past."

Glenna smiled and took her hand and brought her to the table where the tea was waiting.

"Please sit down. I understand."

"Let me change the topic. Now, will we be safe? Your brother will not come and join us. After all you are still in your dressing gown. I thought it would not be appropriate."

"No. We are safe. He has been up for ages. He has a great deal of work to do around the estate and starts very early. He meets with his farm manager, Mr. Kalen. He will join us for breakfast in an hour."

"What time is it?"

"Around nine. We let you sleep as we had such a late night talking last evening."

Molly took a sip of her tea and sighed as she sunk back into her chair.

"Nothing like a really good cuppa. The manager's name is Kalen? K.A.L.E.N."

"Yes, that's right. Mr. Stephen Kalen."

"My father was Sen Kalen. Almost the same. I wonder if he could be a relative of my father. I know nothing about my dad other than his name and that he came from Scotland. I don't even know if he had brothers or sisters."

"Perhaps he might be connected to you."

"Doesn't matter. Nothing ever good came from my father except me and Skye, my mum used to say. That was all she ever said about him." She took another sip. "Nothing like a good cuppa."

"You do sound just like Rachael when you say cuppa."

"I get it. She and I were the same in the future. Loved our tea and chats. Due to the COVID thing, Rachael and Duncan moved back into the castle. Partly because they were worried as she was pregnant. Anna's husband is a doctor you see. Did I tell you that? He arranged for them to have vaccines, and me too, as soon as they could get them. For their staff too. But Rachael didn't want it until the baby was born."

"Vaccinations can be given for smallpox. I assume it is similar?"

"No, I don't think so. I am not sure. Jenner developed the smallpox vaccinations, didn't he?"

"Yes, he did, reduced the disease in London very much. He died earlier this year; I believe. I read it in the newssheet."

"Well, I am not sure how he did it. But in the future, we have two shots of a needle given to us over a few months."

"Sounds better than what Jenner did. He rubbed the sores of the smallpox into a cut or open wound and that would give the person a small dose of the virus."

"All I know is, it is a virus that will kill people, like smallpox and it can be very infectious. Which is another reason I wanted to wait. I went into quarantine and was tested over and over again before I left, to be sure I did not have the virus. I did not want to bring it with me."

"It sounds terrible. Are you sure my brother and the family are safe?"

"I can't be sure, but we have all had the vaccine and it should protect them and me here. And in turn you. I just don't know."

"I would have thought that in the future you would have cured all these diseases."

"Believe me, life is much better than it has been. But diseases and virus change. So, we have to expect changes to occur and do what we can to have a better life. There have been a number of variations of COVID, I think. I am happy they are there. They will be alright, I am sure."

"And I am happy you are here. Now, what do you want to do today? Can you believe you have been here for only a day, and you have shared so much it feels like you have been here a lot longer?"

"It is true. I loved the walk your brother took me on yesterday afternoon. It was lovely to see the castle as it is now and not with all the future additions."

"Does the castle become bigger?"

"Yes, both the castle and the grounds. You will do things... would you mind..."

"I know you want to share that information when Alasdair is around."

"Only the general stuff. I don't want to let either of you miss anything. It is so hard to keep track of what I have told you and what I have not."

"I understand. Can you tell me about your job? A chef. The thought of women having jobs other than being servants seems so unusual."

She emptied her cup and Glenna refilled it.

"I just loved to cook. Mum was always tired when she got home from work so when I was old enough, I offered to prepare some of our meals. You know to give her a break. In our time we didn't have a big house or servants. I guess if we were in this time, we would have been very poor."

"Do not think like that. Just share your excitement in cooking."

"Well, for me it was exciting. I would experiment with different flavours and dishes. Meats and vegies. I also love pastries and cakes. I think I have a bit of a sweet tooth. But I love all sorts of cooking. So, after I finished school, I got an apprenticeship with a famous chef in Melbourne. Mum encouraged it. Then after working with him for three years, and I had finished my apprenticeship, I decided to travel."

"And you did that on your own like Rachael did."

"Yes. I didn't mind. I met lots of great people. I spent time in Greece and on the Island of Corfu. Boy, did I pick up some great recipes there. Then made my way to France. I stayed there for a few months, learning from some wonderful chefs. Then I decided to come to Scotland. I stayed here longer as I just loved the environment. I had only been in Edinburgh a year when the pandemic hit. The rest you know."

"It is remarkable. I mean, a woman travelling around the world like that. I will never be able to do like you, not in this time."

"I guess not but it could be lonely too. I had a few friends and made new ones who I travelled around with, but family were important to me. So, I went home when I could. I just never expected to lose them all within months of each other."

"I am sorry. I did not want to make you sad."

"It's all right. I know I am here for a reason. I don't know why yet, but there you are. One more thing, the maid Morag, why did her smile disappear when she mentioned Rachael?"

"Ahh. Most of the staff, bar a few close retainers, believe Rachael and Duncan died in a shipping accident. It was what we came up with when they decided to go to the future. A few days after they left, we got the news of a shipwreck. We used it to our advantage. It is not a nice thing, but it stopped difficult questions being asked."

"I will ask you later who I need to be careful around. I don't want to put my foot in it."

Glenna gave her a peculiar look and then shook her head.

"So, shall we have a walk after breakfast? I can tell you then."

"Yes, then I want to ask Alasdair if he will teach me to ride."

"I will leave you to dress," she pointed to a day dress slung over the chair on the other side of the room, "and I will see about a riding outfit for you."

"Sounds like you have an outfit for every occasion."

"I do and a spare." She laughed and left the room.

Again, the maid, Morag, helped her to dress, and she was pondering the strangeness of the situation, as she made her way to the dining room. As she drew close, she heard her name being called. She turned to see Alasdair making his way to her. She waited for him to catch up.

"Come this way, my dear," he offered her his arm. "We have a breakfast room."

"Of course, you do." She smiled at him, and his face brightened.

They turned the other way from the dining room and entered what she assumed was the breakfast room. Glenna was already seated, having another cup of tea.

He escorted her to the table and pulled a chair out for her. She sat. A cup of tea was placed in front of her. He sat down next to her.

The room was light and airy. The furniture all white. So different from the dining room with its mahogany table and dark furnishings. The room was making her come alive. Waking her up for the new day ahead. She liked the breakfast room a lot.

"Coffee for me, MacGregor."

"You aren't a tea drinker?"

"Yes and no. I love to drink coffee in the morning and tea in the afternoon and evening."

"Interesting. I have some lovely coffee cake recipes I could make for you."

"Cake with coffee in them. Mmmmm. Sounds delightful." He smiled.

She took a sip of her tea and looked at Glenna who was grinning at her from across the table. Best she jumped into her new life as quickly as she could. So, she did.

"Alasdair, I was wondering if you had time to teach me how to ride."

"You are serious, then."

"Yes. I believe the experience will be good for me."

"I think you may be right. How about we go to the stables after breakfast and have our first lesson."

She glanced at Glenna who gave her no indication as to if she had found her a riding outfit. Glenna must have read her mind.

"I have an outfit that will be ready for her to use tomorrow."

"Wonderful. Then we will go to the stables this morning for the most important lesson of all."

She looked into his eyes but could not guess what he meant.

"You need to become acquainted with your horse. We will need to find one just right for you."

She smiled. "Ahh. I understand. Let him become acquainted with who I am. What I am like. My voice etc."

"Exactly. I believe Miss Molly that you will learn quickly and will enjoy being a horse woman."

"I hope you are right. It sounds like a wonderful pastime."

"This is Greta. She is a four-year-old mare. She is very gentle and is a loving animal. She loves to be petted. I thought she might be right for you."

Molly placed her hand on Greta's forehead. And slowly moved closer to her. Greta nuzzled into her. They became friends immediately. Stroking her nose, she drew even closer.

"You are a beautiful girl." She whispered. "I want us to be friends." Greta gently nodded.

Molly stepped back to smile at this beautiful creature. Greta was a ginger or pale chestnut. *Yes chestnut.* She had never heard the colour ginger applied to a horse. She had a streak of white running down her nose and around her mouth. Her mane was blonde and shining. In Molly's eyes, she was a beautiful horse.

"I love the way the white comes down her nose and around her mouth."

"Her muzzle."

"Muzzle?"

"Yes, that's what you call this part of the horse." He handed her a carrot which she promptly placed near Greta's muzzle, and she ate hungrily.

"Would you like to lead her around."

"Can I?"

A stable boy came over and attached a bridle to Greta and then handed her the reins. This took a minute or two, so she examined her newfound friend as closely as possible. Such a gentle animal.

Slowly she pulled on the reins and drew her out of her stall. Greta followed her out into the yard.

"I think she likes me."

"I believe you are correct. You have found a new friend. Come out and see her when you can. She can become familiar with your voice, and I am sure you will both enjoy each other's company."

Molly walked her around the yard a few times, stopping every now and then to whisper something into her ear. Greta would nod her head and nuzzle into her.

"This is truly amazing. I grew up in the city. I have never seen a horse up close like this before. Let alone ride one."

"Then tomorrow you will have a first experience here in the past, I hope you will learn to love."

"Oh, I hope so too. Thank you, Alasdair. I look forward to learning all I can. Thank you for picking Greta for me."

He smiled at her, and her stomach did a somersault. She was sure she was grinning like the Cheshire cat, but she didn't care. This was a delight that lifted her spirits. She liked the horse, and she loved the way Alasdair made her feel all gooey inside.

The stable boy came over to take Greta from her.

"Can I take her back?"

The boy looked at his master who nodded.

"Yes miss." He replied.

She led Greta back into the stable. And took her into her stall. It had enough room in the stall that she could turn Greta around and then she handed the reins back to the stable boy.

"Well done, Molly. You and Greta are a team. You are doing well. Now let us go in. You need to change your slippers and I will get one of the servants to find you some fine ladies riding boots."

Molly looked down at her slippers and was concerned that she had ruined them. They were covered in dirt and wet also.

"I am sorry. I should have thought..."

"No need to apologise. It can be easily fixed."

They walked to the rear of the castle and found a seat near the kitchen door.

She sat down and was about to remove her slipper when she found Alasdair kneeling in front of her.

He lifted her foot and gently pulled her slipper off.

Her stomach did another somersault. His hand was warm on her stockinged ankle. He lifted her other foot as a maid came out the door. He took off the second slipper and handed the slippers to the maid and asked her to have them cleaned.

Her head was spinning, and her face was heating up.

"I suggest, my dear, that you return to your room and change your stockings. And please return to the library when you are ready and join me for tea."

"And coffee."

"Yes, I will have coffee." He added and took her hand and escorted her to the stairs.

She went upstairs and fell onto her bed. His charisma was getting to her. She had to be careful. Alasdair was not the type to take any woman seriously, was he? Women were fun for him. Well, at least when Rachael was here. So far, she had not seen the man Rachael had described. He was not the man she had envisioned. So perhaps she needed to rethink. One thing she did know was she had to stop reacting to him. Somersaults in stomachs would have to stop.

9

WHAT MORE NEEDED TO BE SAID?

1823

After tea she spent the afternoon with Glenna, sorting out some of Rachael's dresses and seeing what could be altered and used for her. But she could not get Alasdair out of her mind. She decided to ask some pointed questions of Glenna, in part to get to know her better but also to work out if Alasdair was...she couldn't think what he was.

"Well, I believe we have all you need."

"Not quite. Underwear." Her eyebrows lifted as she gazed at Glenna, with her arms placed firmly on her hips.

"Yes. I thought you might have the same problem Rachael had." She gave a little giggle. "I have had some underpants made for you, similar to the design that Rachael gave us."

She walked over to the chest of draws and took a small pile off the top.

"These should suit. I am having more made for you."

She handed them to Molly.

"They are soft. And look about right."

Molly placed them on the bed next to some of her dresses and then went to sit down at the table where Glenna was ticking something on a paper list she had.

"Can I ask you some personal questions, please?"

"Of course, my dear Molly. Ask, what is worrying you?"

"Well, nothing is really worrying me..."

"I would say the concern written on your face is a worry. What can I help you with?"

"It's Alasdair."

Glenna smiled. "You had a different opinion of him when you arrived. Am I right?"

"Yes, but he does not fulfil that description anymore."

"I think it is safe to say your thoughts of him were coloured by the experiences of Rachael."

Molly lowered her head and stared at her feet. "I know now I shouldn't have let that happen, but yes, you are right."

"Do not fret. I understand how Rachael felt but I also have seen the change in my brother since... Well in this past year. He has taken his responsibilities very seriously and put away childish behaviour and thoughts. You could say you are meeting the new and improved version of Alasdair."

"I do understand. And he is different than what I expected. But I am concerned at my reaction to him. I am moved by his thoughts and his love for his family and the estate. I have been here a short time, but I can't get him out of my head."

Glenna smiled and placed her hand in Molly's. "If it is meant to be then relax and enjoy those thoughts. He is a worthy man. And you will determine for yourself if he is worthy of you."

"But I am not thinking like...I am not worthy. I am fragile, unsure of what I want. I'm in the past for heaven's sake. Who am I to be falling in love with anyone? Especially here."

"Molly, do not underestimate yourself. Just enjoy your time

here. If you happen to develop a deeper relationship with Alasdair, then you can question yourself. But just enjoy the time you have. This is an opportunity few get to experience. The fae have chosen you for a reason. It might take some time to find the reason, that's all."

"Glenna, you have a great deal of wisdom. I wish I could think like you. I still have difficulty believing I am even here."

"There is nothing wrong with your own wisdom. You had recognised the change in him. Few would have taken the time to notice. Thank you."

"So, the bulk of what we discussed and prepared I have shared with you. I think I would like to just enjoy my time here. I will answer any questions you have and discuss anything with you but either alone or perhaps just at dinner. Like we are doing now."

"That makes a great deal of sense, Molly dear. I do want you to relax and get to know us as we are, here and now."

"Thank you, Glenna. And how do you feel about it, Alasdair?"

"Miss Molly, you have brought us such joy and hope for my family in the future. I agree we should limit out future discussions to when we are here having dinner or perhaps in private. I hope you noticed I dismissed the staff from here the moment we sat down."

"I did, Alasdair. Thank you."

"We know you wish to learn to ride. What else would you like to do."

"Well, I guess I would like to spend time with your cook, Mrs. Gillies."

"And..."

"I would love to spend time with you as you do your work on the estate. Meet some of the people who work with you."

"If you would like I would be happy for you to accompany me."

She watched his face colour slightly. He smiled and then coughed.

"Thank you." She returned a smile.

"We plan to go to Edinburgh to catch up with our other brother, later in the month. Shall we all go together, and you can see how the city is in our time?"

"Oh yes please. That would be delightful."

"Then it is settled. Is there anything else?"

"I would just like to ride, when I am able, around the estate and see the countryside for myself."

"This we can arrange but a stable hand will travel with you when I or Glenna cannot. For your safety, of course."

"Sounds most sensible."

"Then all is settled. After dinner I would like to relax in the library and just enjoy your company. I want to hear more about you. Your likes and dislikes. Things you like and make you happy. Of course, only if you will allow me, to know you better."

"I would be delighted." And she was. She wanted to get to know this man better. "Thank you."

"This has been a wonderful day."

"It has, Molly. I will make sure you have the chance to sleep in, and we can arrange all the clothing into your room in the morning."

"Thank you, Glenna, for all you have done. I feel very lucky to be in this place."

"You are most welcome. Then brother, you might like to take Molly to your meeting with the manager, Mr. Kalen."

"I would be delighted."

"I am off to bed. But Molly, stay and fill my brother in on what you know of your father. He may know more of the manager's family background. It might help you."

Then Glenna was gone, and she sat next to Alasdair, alone, her stomach doing somersaults, again.

So much for control.

"What is this about your father?"

"Well, I don't know a lot about him. His name was Sen Kalen, and he came from Scotland. But he left us when I was only three. I have no real memory of him. Just a blur. I only have a photo that was taken of him with us just before he disappeared. I will show you later. It is in my room." She lowered her head and examined her feet.

"I cannot imagine anyone who would leave his wife and children alone."

"I know. Even though it is common in our time it is strange he has never tried to reconnect. It made me imagine he was dead. It felt better if I thought he was."

"Kalen is an unusual name. So, I imagine you are wondering if our Mr. Kalen might be an ancestor of yours?"

"Yes. It's a long shot but you never know." She looked at the ring that was her mother's. The ring her father had given her. It was the only thing her mother kept. She even got rid of her wedding ring. But not the sapphire. "I imagine he knows nothing of the time travel."

"Mr. Kalen is a very unusual man. If he does, he has made no attempt to discuss it with me. He is a very quiet man. He does the job of managing the land very well. But he and I do not always see eye to eye. Especially with the changes we have made to the estate, thanks to the prompting of Rachael."

"Rachael told me of those suggestions. Have you implemented any yet?"

"Yes. We got our distillery ready to start producing whisky and just a few months ago the government in London allowed us to export and pay a tax. Just as she said they would. We have been ahead of the rest of Scotland and already we can see the benefits of our whisky being sent around the world. A very worthwhile investment in our future."

"That part of the plan included your brother Hamish?"

"Yes, and I will be delighted to introduce you to him when we go to Edinburgh. He loves our import and export business. He was so well suited to that part of my father's business. He loves to travel the world."

He picked up her hand. And her stomach was somersaulting again.

"I do not want you to fret over your lineage. The fae think highly of you, or you would not be here."

"It is not my lineage as such, it is more the unanswered questions of my past and may never get answered. I know so little of my father and his roots."

"I think I understand." His thumb rubbed back and forth over her knuckles. Even now he was concerned for her.

"Thank you, Alasdair."

"Molly..."

"You want to ask me something?"

"Yes. Would you please call me Dair?"

"That is an endearment."

"It is. And you have become very dear to me."

"But we barely know each other."

"I know more about you than I know of any woman. And I am

glad of it. We know how to talk with each other. Yes, it has been quick. But I am not foolish enough to ignore the fact you have come to the past for a reason. And I hope the reason is me."

Her head was spinning. She had feelings for Alasdair she could not deny. He had sensed them in her as well. Perhaps...

He leaned in and kissed her gently on the lips. He moved closer. He wrapped his arms softly around her and drew her closer to him.

The kiss deepened and she was lost. Lost in the rapture and passion that was Dair. Her Dair. She knew it. He was for her and she for him.

He gently pulled away looking into her eyes. She could see him in the depths of his eyes. She was captured and was exhilarated. Could she actually be in love with this man? Yes, she could see she had been falling for him since she first heard of him from Rachael.

"My dearest Molly. I tell you true. I have never felt so complete as I do now with your arms around me. Could your coming mean I might have a chance at love? To love you, my beautiful wonderous Molly?"

"My head says this is going too quickly, but my heart wants you to hold me and kiss me like this forever."

He let his forehead rest on hers.

"I promise I will not push you. I will allow you time to become accustomed to me. To fall in love with me. But I will not let you go, Molly. I want us to be together and when you are ready, my wife."

"Your wife?"

"If you want to stay and be with me."

She stood and he stood. She wrapped her arms around him. She felt his arm gently encircle her. She held him and he her.

"I will say goodnight. I have a lot to think about."

"Very well. But I will see you at breakfast and I want you to sit with me."

"Very well, Dair."

He smiled and hugged her again then let her go.

She was sure she floated to her bedroom, her feet never touching the ground, not once. This was right. This was why she was here. For him and for herself.

10

YOU HAVE GOT TO BE KIDDING!

The maid, Lizzie, brought her tea and had opened her curtains. She had slept the sweet dreams of love. She was refreshed and excited all at once. She got up and placed her dressing gown on. Glenna knocked and came and sat down with her.

"My dear friend, you have a smile as big as... My brother loves you."

"He does. I can't deny it. I thought it could not be possible after such a short length of time, but it is. I can see how love at first sight is possible."

Glenna leaned back in her seat. "I do not doubt it. I saw similar in Duncan. He denied his feelings for some time, however. But has my Dair returned your feelings in truth?"

"Yes. I can barely believe it myself. But he has no doubt I was sent by the fae for him. How can we be attracted so quickly, I don't understand? But there have been others who have loved at first sight. Perhaps it is true."

"This is wonderful. He was convinced love was going to pass

him by. For him to say he loves you... But it would seem the fae have other ideas."

Was this a fae trick?

She knew she could trust the answer that Glenna gave her, so she asked. "But do we love each other or is this some kind of spell the fae have used?"

"Do not place that sin against the fae. They might give a situation a helping hand, but the people involved make the decisions. If you love him and have declared it and he love you and has done the same, then you do not need to doubt. You love each other."

"Again, your wisdom amazes me, Glenna. You know what I am thinking before I do. Thank you."

"Today will be a remarkable day." She sat forward and poured the tea.

"I do believe you are right." She smiled at Glenna, her skin tingling at their unique connection too. "Today is a special day."

Molly and Glenna entered the breakfast room together, but he only had eyes for Molly. Her beauty was real. Her smile and her kisses for him. His heart was beating harder, and his breath caught. To think such a wonderful future lady could be for him. Especially as he had treated Rachael so badly. And had kept poor Delia on a string. But he could not deny his feelings for Molly as they washed all over him.

He stood and offered his hand to Molly. She came and took it. They both smiled at Glenna who was beaming with delight. He pulled out the chair for her and she sat. He sat next to her as Glenna took the seat opposite them.

"I am delighted for you both. I can see this is so right. You are both wonderful people who deserve love and I could not be more delighted."

"Thank you, sister." He took Molly's hand and lifted her fingers to his lips and kissed them.

"It is a dream come true. One, I had not expected but accept with open arms."

He lifted Molly's hand again and pressed his lips to her fingers. "Molly, I have a surprise." He then turned to his sister. "Glenna, will you deal with the estate for the next week? I want to spend every waking moment with Molly."

"Certainly."

"I want us to talk and find out all we need to know about each other. I know this experience has been quick, but it feels so right." He placed his hand on his heart. "Here, where it matters."

Molly turned to face him.

"This is a wonderful idea. You can teach me to ride still, can't you?"

"Of course, and we can go on picnics and go into Aberlour. I just want us to be together with no distraction. So, we do not doubt what we are feeling."

"What a wonderful idea. I would love it."

"Then it is settled. We will go for a walk after breakfast and work out what we will do for the week. I have no doubt we can see a great deal of the estate as we go."

"I will meet with Mr. Kalen and fill him in with your plans."

"Thank you, Glenna."

"It is my pleasure. I hope you will enjoy yourselves. I look forward to our evening meals and you telling me of the day you both have had."

"I am sure we will." He smiled at Molly who blushed a brighter shade of red than she had already. He wanted to know everything he could about her.

"Now what has cook prepared for us today?" He rubbed his hands together.

The footman brought over a tureen which contained porridge.

"Is this proper Scottish porridge?"

He watched Molly become animated. "Well, no. Cook has developed her own recipe which is a family favourite. It is cooked in milk and then smothered in honey. And we top it off with a sprinkling of cinnamon and brown sugar." Even speaking the words were making his mouth water. The footman placed some on Molly's and his plates.

"Where does the brown sugar come from?"

"Hamish has it imported from the Caribbean. It is very popular."

Molly picked up a spoon and had a taste. She closed her eyes and swooned. That's what she did, she swooned.

"That has to be the best porridge I have ever tasted."

She closed her eyes as she took another mouthful.

He adored how she absorbed her senses in the tasting of her food.

The footman placed the tureen on the table and fetched the rest of the food.

"We also have eggs, potato cakes and fresh bread, sir."

"Thank you, MacGregor."

Another footman placed all the food on the table in front of them. MacGregor poured tea for each of the ladies. Then poured coffee for him.

"Thank you, both. We will call you when we are ready." And dismissed the footmen.

"I am really enjoying the food. I might have to have a run if I put on weight."

"Rachael did that." Added Glenna. "She loved to run. A very unusual pastime."

"I am not a fitness fanatic, but I try to be careful when I do eat too much and have to 'work it off'." She smiled at him, and he could not contain his joy. He began to laugh, not at her but with her, and she soon joined in.

"I am sure our walks around the estate will help you to 'work off' as Rachael used to say, your enjoyment of food. But I can show you where Rachael used to run and not be disturbed."

"You know, I think you might be right. Walking and a private run. Sounds great. Bring on more breakfasts like this. I'm ready for it." Her laugh echoed around the room.

"So, what things would you like to ask me?" He wrapped his hand in hers.

"Please tell me about your childhood. And your mum. What was her name?"

He loved the feel of her skin and the warmth of her embrace. Holding her hand was special.

"My mother was fae, I now know. She was beautiful. She was Jean Buchanan."

"Jean, like Clara's middle name. That makes sense."

"Yes, I am delighted Duncan and Rachael used her name. Mother fell in love with our father and decided to stay here with him." His eyes were looking into the distance as he remembered his mother.

"It's like a fairy tale. Was she happy?"

"Yes. She had Duncan, then me and Hamish. When Glenna was born, she felt her life was complete, I think. She loved my father and all of us. But as the line of fae only happens in the females of mixed marriages, she was especially excited when

Glenna was born. Mind you, I thought it was just because she had a daughter. The fae meant nothing to me then."

"So, when a fae marries a mortal, the females are the only ones born with the magic?"

"Yes, that's right. Glenna has the magic."

"Wow, that makes so much more sense to me. Her wisdom. That is her magic."

"Glenna was in part responsible for me accepting the reality of the fae. She never stopped reminding me of the stories and of what Mother would think."

"But you accepted the fact when Rachael went back to the future?"

"Yes. I saw her disappear in the teal blue light of the fae. I have never forgotten the moment. It was then all the stories mother and Glenna had told, fell into place, and it all became real."

"I can imagine the shock it must have been. For me it was feeling the healing power within me, the fae had given me, without my even asking. I'm not fae but they seem real to me."

"But you believe."

"Yes, but mainly from hearing Rachael's story and knowing what had happened to her was in a way happening to me. Just under different circumstances. And I had no idea you were going to be part of the story or part of my healing."

They both were silent for a moment as they took in the words they had spoken.

"Thank you for the boots. They are perfect and so very comfortable. Even walking on the grass was damaging the slippers."

"You are more than welcome, Molly. You are dearer to me than you can imagine."

"Can you tell me what it is of me...? I mean, what is it that you..."

"Love?"

She nodded, then set her eyes to the ground.

He stopped and lifted her chin.

He examined her eyes. Bluer than blue. The mirror into her soul and his.

"I love your eyes. You do not hide behind them. I can see truth, love, and sadness in them. You let me look inside you through your eyes. Thank you. I also love your hair." He touched her curls and wound one around his finger. "You are beautiful."

She lowered her head again. He again lifted her chin. "But it is not just your beautiful face. It is you. You are caring. Your main concern when you arrived, was for us. The photos, the discussions with Duncan and Rachael. You wanted Glenna and I to be happy. To know in our hearts, they are happy in the future. You took it upon yourself to share them before anything else."

"It was so important for you to know."

"Thank you. It is a beautiful thought. That is what makes you beautiful."

"I have been told I am beautiful, but I have taken no notice. I want people to love the inside of me not the outside. Does that make sense?"

"Yes, but it is clear to all who know you, your beauty comes from within. I see and I am sure Glenna does too. As did Rachael and Duncan."

"Thank you."

"Honestly, it is my pleasure." They continued their walk. But he had to ask his question. "What are you attracted to in me? I know you thought me different to begin with."

"You are right. I thought you would be selfish, self-absorbed and would see me just as someone you could take advantage of."

"My faults by your eyes make me a blackguard."

"Yes, I imagine they do. But I watched you and listened to you.

Your concern for your brother and Rachael. Your self-condemnation of your actions against Rachael. Your keen awareness for their happiness. These things showed me another side to the man I had prejudged. I had no right to do that, and I am sorry."

"I understand. And you need not apologise. I would say we can see the real person within our skins."

"This is so unfamiliar to me. I have never felt so comfortable with any man around me. I like men, don't get me wrong but I was so busy with work I had no time for a boyfriend. And none attracted me to them. But being here with you feels so right. I feel the same way I did when I woke up on the hill. Refreshed, renewed and happy. Does it make sense to you?"

"In a funny way it does. I wanted to be at peace about the decisions we made, and I wanted a mate. Ask Glenna. I felt I did not deserve one. But it's as if you are the answer to my concerns. And I was attracted to you immediately. Believe me. The moment I caught you as you fainted, up on the hill, I was smitten. It was so unexpected. I haven't been able to look at a woman for a year now. Because..."

"Because of Rachael."

"Yes."

"Then let me say something. Let us forget the past. Think only of a future, a future with each other here in the past."

"You are beautiful and have just proven it again to me. I agree."

"So, my dear Dair, let's go to the stable. You have to teach me to ride."

"Good morning, Miss Glenna."

"Good morning Mr. Kalen. I hope you don't mind if you deal with me for the next week. My brother is busy with a guest we have staying with us."

"No problem at all, miss."

Glenna sat in the chair behind the desk where she had seen her brothers sit many times. She directed Mr. Kalen to sit.

"I am sure we can manage."

He was a pleasant man. In his fifties but very fit for a man his age. He was handsome but she noted she had never seen the man smile. His hair was dark brown with the light flicker of greys in among his curls. She had always wondered why he had never married.

"Now is there anything specific we should deal with?"

"Only the cows, miss."

"Cows?"

"Yes. I plan to take them to the other side of the river for this coming week. Just to vary their diet from the grasses to the wild-flower meadow."

"Very well." She made a note. She also noted Mr. Kalen could not sit still in his chair. He was constantly adjusting the way he sat.

"Saw the young lady visiting yesterday, having a look at the horses. Is she happy with Greta?"

"I do believe she is, Mr. Kalen. Her father was a Kalen."

"Is that a fact. What are the chances of that?" A gentle smile lifted his lips.

"I said the exact same thing. Your surname is not very common."

"No, it is not miss. What is her father's first name?"

"It too is unusual. Sen, I believe."

The man paled. "Sen you say. I have a distant relation with the same name."

"I must introduce you to Molly at some time."

He paled again. She did not think it was possible for him to look paler, but he was.

"Molly Kalen?"

"No actually, it is Molly Grace. She took her mother's maiden name, I believe."

Mr. Kalen stood.

"If you will excuse me miss, I will see you tomorrow. I just remembered I need to check on one of the cows, who is with calf."

He turned and left the room before she could utter a goodbye. He seemed distracted and sad and out of sorts. She made a mental note to seek him out later in the day to see if he was alright. What had upset him? Something had and so suddenly. And it was obviously related to the name Kalen and Molly Grace. There was more going on here than she could put her finger on.

11

FIRST RIDING LESSON AND MORE

Day One

After their walk yesterday, Dair had decided today they would have her first riding lesson. Glenna had given her a green riding outfit. She was loving all the outfits Glenna had arranged for her. Dair was telling her she could get more when they went to Edinburgh. She did not doubt him. But for now, her first lesson had gone very well. She had taken to the side saddle as she knew no other way to ride. They had ridden for two hours around the flat areas of the estate.

"No hills for you yet, my dear. You have done so very well. But you will find your muscles will ache as you have not ridden before. So, we will stay on the flat."

And her darling Dair was right. When he had lifted her off her horse, back at the stable, she could barely move. He took her hand and gently walked her the long way into the house. This allowed her muscles to loosen, at least a little bit.

After luncheon she met Mrs. Gillies, the cook, and they immediately hit it off. She showed her the kitchen and all the fine modern gadgets the Murrays had supplied. Mrs. Gillies showed her how they made cream and she was fascinated. And by her side was Dair watching her every move and laughing and enjoying her discoveries. She squealed with joy; she was so happy.

Many of the other servants came and went from the kitchen. More came than went when she produced several batches of cookies. Dair also enjoyed watching her and eating her wares. She was having so much fun.

Watching his beloved enjoy her time in the kitchen gave him so much joy. She threw herself into learning all she could from Mrs. Gillies. And he loved to be there. He was sitting in his office on the other side of the castle. Molly had gone to freshen up. He had made a list of things he wanted to do with her and was ticking off what they had already done. Now he was writing down what they had already discussed.

He leaned back in his chair and thoughts of his father flitted through him, not for the first time.

What would his father think of him now being the laird? And would he approve of Molly? He pondered and could hear his father's voice in his mind.

"Son, this is your place. Duncan was the heir, but I am so pleased he found love with Rachael. Now it is your turn. You are a good laird. And Molly is a beautiful soul. Be happy, my lad. This is what is meant to be..."

He looked up at the painting of his father as a young man. He could see his eyes smiling down at him. Yes, this was all as it should be. He knew Molly wanted what they had but was occasionally overwhelmed at the fast pace it had taken. He did not doubt her love for him for a moment. But he could see she struggled with the timing.

There was a knock at the door. Molly popped her head around the door.

"Can I disturb you for a moment?"

"Dearest Molly, you can come to me anytime you need to talk to me or just see me. It will never disturb me."

She came in and sat in the seat opposite him.

"I was thinking about the conversation we had about your mother, and I was keen to ask you some questions about your dad. Or as the Scots say *Da.*"

"I was just thinking of my father. Funny you should ask. We seldom called him da. Father was just the way we always addressed him."

"What was his name? His given name."

"Duncan Callum Malcom Lucas Murray."

"Boy he had heaps of names. Do you have as many? What are all yours?"

"Alasdair Peter Fergus Ross. And brother Hamish is Hamish Wallace Duncan MacArthur. And Glenna is Glenna Jean Maree Alvina."

"What about your brother Duncan?"

"Almost exactly like my father. Duncan Callum Malcom Jasper Murray."

"Wow and do all the names have special significance?"

"Yes. Each name comes from an ancestor who held a special place in the family or clan Murray. For example, Alasdair is named for my grandfather, Peter was a great uncle, Fergus a brother of a family member around two hundred years ago and Ross was my father's best friend."

"I will have to learn the names of the ancestors and well..."

Alasdair stood and came to kneel before her.

"There is room for new names to be added to the family tree if you are wondering. Yes, we like to continue with tradition, but we also like to imagine names for new individuals, like Molly for example."

She was beaming at him and leaned forward and kissed him. Oh, her lips were warm and soft. He held her close and deepened the kiss. He wanted this woman with every inch of his body. He slowly pulled away.

Resting his forehead on hers, he asked, "Was there anything else."

She sighed, "Yes but I am happy to wait. I was mainly curious about his name. I knew Jean and wanted to know his. I should have guessed he was a Duncan. Thanks for the info."

"You are most welcome."

"I think I will go and read in the library before we have afternoon tea."

"I think that is a fine idea. I will come and show you where all the family history is so you can see for yourself where we fit in, in this clan."

"That's a lovely idea."

She put out her hand to him and he took it giving it a little squeeze, closing the door to his study as they went.

12

LET'S COOK

Day Three

"I must admit I am enjoying all we have been doing. But watching you cook has been sensational."

"That's because you think servants have to do these things. Well, they don't. Do they, Mrs. Gillies?"

"Very true, Miss Molly. Every wife, no matter what her station in life, should learn to cook."

"Because it's fun."

"Again, *verrry* true miss."

Molly laughed out loud. She loved spending time with Mrs. Gillies and listening to her broad Scottish accent. They had shared so many tips already and Dair was there with her watching her have fun. She had not cooked for so long before she had come here.

Many of the staff would come by the kitchen to watch her if they had the opportunity. And specially to sample her chocolate chip cookies and the peanut butter melting moments. She had learned to adjust to this not so modern world. They had no idea what peanut butter was. She soon learned what to do and how to make it from scratch. Chocolate came in enormous blocks, but she soon learned how to turn some of it into chips for the cookies.

Today she was making scones, Scottish style, and the traditional recipe she knew was not yet a big thing but was also having a go at. The Scottish style was a bit rougher, using not so fine flour. Bigger bits of oats floated through the mixture. Mrs. Gillies was explaining...

"And when we have cooked them, we serve it with lovely honey."

"Whereas we serve it with jam and cream. But as you can see my flour is so much finer than yours."

"That it is, *deary*."

"And I cannot wait to taste them both." Dair added laughing at the joy he saw on both ladies faces.

Molly smiled and began to sing. Well, it was more of a hum. She was sure not to mention any words. She was humming a modern song after all. But she soon stopped as Mrs. Gillies began to sing. And oh, what a wonderful voice the dear lady had.

The Elfin knight stands on yon hill,
Blaw, blaw, blaw winds, blaw
Blawing his horn loud and shrill.
And the wind has blawin my plaid awa

If I had yon horn in my kist,
Blaw, blaw, blaw winds, blaw
And the bonny laddie here that I luve best!
And the wind has blawin my plaid awa
Ye maun make me a fine Holland sark

.

Blaw, blaw, blaw winds, blaw
Without ony stitching or needle wark.
And the wind has blawin my plaid awa
And ye maun wash it in yonder well,

Blaw, blaw, blaw winds, blaw
Where the dew never wat, nor the rain ever fell.
And the wind has blawin my plaid awa
Now sin ye've askd some things o me,

Blaw, blaw, blaw winds, blaw
It's right I ask as mony o thee.
And the wind has blawin my plaid awa

My father he askd me an acre o land,
Blaw, blaw, blaw winds, blaw
Between the saut sea and the strand.
And the wind has blawin my plaid awa

And ye maun plow 't wi your blawing horn,
Blaw, blaw, blaw winds, blaw
And ye maun saw 't wi pepper corn.
And the wind has blawin my plaid awa

• • •

When ye've dune, and finishd your wark,
Blaw, blaw, blaw winds, blaw
Ye'll come to me, luve, and get your sark.
And the wind has blawin my plaid awa"

She was applauding and some of the servants joined in. "Oh, Mrs Gillies that was wonderful. But some of it I didn't understand. Can you explain a few things for me?"

"Of course, *my dear*. What do you wish to know?"

"What is a sark?"

"A shirt my dear, like one your Dair is wearing."

"Blaw is blow?"

"Yes, my dear, it is."

"Now what were some...kist?"

"That is simple my dear. A chest, where you store your sark."

He watched as She laughed. joy filling every part of her. "I love this language. I want to learn more. Please sing it again Mrs. Gillies."

And she did and by then the scones were on a tray ready to be placed in the oven. They tidied the kitchen while they were waiting for them to cook and both she and Mrs. Gillies were humming the *Elfin knight*.

One of the assistants to cook, had whipped the cream till it was almost like butter. Molly placed a finger in and took a bit to taste. She was swooning as her Dair would say as she tasted the wonderful treat. Mrs. Gillies had opened her vast larder to Molly so that she could see all the jams available to her to serve with her scones. Mrs. Gillies had picked the honey and Molly had taken out a jar of strawberry jam, gooseberry jam and redcurrant jam. All of which she could hardly wait to taste.

"Now Dair, *me deary, ye* can be the judge."

"Now Mrs. Gillies, that is hardly fair, as I wish to keep both you lovely ladies happy. And do not giggle at me Miss Molly, or you may be extremely disappointed."

She placed her scone in front of him and Mrs. Gillies did also. The honey oozed over the brownish warm scone. He took a bite and she grinned as she watched him swoon with his eyes tightly closed.

"Best Scottish scone I have ever tasted." He said when his mouth was empty of food.

"Now for this interloper..." He raised his eyebrow at her, and she could not stop smiling.

He took a bite as she placed her hands on her hips and looked very carefully at his face, awaiting the reaction. He swooned, which was a good sign. He licked the strawberry jam and cream from his lips.

"I have to admit I have not tasted anything quite like this."

"*Noor haavee I.*" came the muffled voice of Mrs. Gillies, as she too licked her lips.

"I think we can safely call it a tie. Would you not agree, my dear?"

And she burst into joyous laughter.

"Yes!" she said and clapped with all the other kitchen staff.

They enjoyed riding every day but for him the kitchen had become a new place for adventure. Molly was in her element. This was where he could see the joy food and preparing it gave her. Mrs. Gillies was so welcoming to her and wanted to learn from her. But that was what Molly wanted too. He grinned every time a new piece of information was revealed to her. She was like a small child watch a butterfly escape the cocoon.

"No *deary*, try the honey on top of the meat."

Molly took a bite of the honeyed veal. She closed her eyes and swooned. Little mmm's and ohhhs came from her. She swallowed.

"That has to be the best meat on the planet. Mrs. Gillies, you and honey are my new favourite things."

"*Ye* spoil me, miss." And the lady blushed a deep crimson.

"But it's true. I had no idea honey could be used in so many ways."

"*Aye*, honey is a gift from the almighty. We need to make good use of it."

"Thank you for your time, Mrs. Gillies. I will take the lovely Molly as I have a surprise for her."

"Surprise? This is exciting. Do I need to change?"

"No, my darling. Just freshen up and meet me out the front. And bring a cloak to wear as we will be going on a curricle ride."

"Oh, this is grand. Give me a moment. I won't be long." She turned and dashed out the kitchen.

"Well Master Alasdair, you have found a wonderful woman."

"I have. She is all I have ever dreamed of and more. I just hope and pray she will stay and marry me."

"*Aye*, she is a catch but then so are you."

He turned his head and grinned at the cook. He had great affection for her. She was a loyal and trusted clan member and friend.

"Thank you, Mrs. Gillies. I appreciate it."

13

SURPRISE

Day Five

They were making their way down a smooth dirt track at the southern edge of the estate, toward the closest point to the river Spey. He knew she would like what he had created for her. It had only taken a few days to organise, and he had used clan members and staff who knew the fae secrets. Cuddled up in her cloak she leaned into him trying to stay warm.

"I am so excited about the surprise. I have no idea what you are doing. But I love curricle riding. You can add that to the list of things I like here in the past."

"I hope you will find my token gift to your liking."

"Token gift? Now I am intrigued."

He pulled the carriage up near a wood where the dirt track ended. Helping her down from the curricle he could not help but notice the curiosity in her eyes. Taking her hand, he led her to a path that drew them into the wood. Soon the trees blocked the view of the open field of the estate where they had pulled up. She looked up into his eyes, trusting but curious. They continued to walk until a post came into view. On top of that post was a '0', carved into the side.

She stopped and placed her fingers on the '0'. "What is this?"

"I have created a track that goes through the wood, which you can use to exercise. In private, so the modern exercises you want to do will not bring the eyes of strangers down on top of you."

"Really? I can't believe it."

"I remember that Rachael would sneak out early in the morning to run. But she was always worried that she would reveal more of her future self."

"I think I understand."

"Let me show you." He held her hand as they continued to walk down the path, which was now getting wider. The vegetation had been removed and the path flattened. It was just plain dirt but smooth. He kept looking at her face to watch her reactions, as they walked. At one point he made the comment about the smoothness of the surface.

After some minutes they came to another post. This one had a '1' carved in the top on the side also. They kept walking in the silence, and he watched her carefully. Her smile widened every time they came to a new post. In all five posts she had seen. The last post was the other side of the first post that had the '0' marked on it.

"Am I correct, the path is five miles long and winds its way through this forest?"

"Yes, that is right. Are you pleased?"

"Pleased? I'm amazed that you would do this for me."

"I want you to be happy. I thought this might give you the incentive to exercise. Something you like to do, and you might miss if you came to live in the past."

She reached up and kissed him.

"And..." He sighed, "you might let me come and run with you."

"Yes please. I would love you to. Really love you to."

What an incredible gift. She stared into his eyes as they glowed in the soft light of the forest. She was falling for him even more than before. He did all this for her. He had said he had worked out the course and had trusted friends and servants create the path and lay soft soil on the top of it.

It was beautiful and the trees hid it from the view of those he did not want to see it. This was such a special gift and it overwhelmed her.

He took her hand and led her back to the curricle.

Before he helped her back in, she hugged him. He kissed her on the top of her head.

"I would do anything for you." He whispered

"Thank you, Dair. It means everything to me. Would you watch me do one lap?"

"Now? But you are hardly dressed for it."

"I know but if you don't mind, I can take the dress off and run in my underwear."

"If you wish."

"I know this is not very lady like, but I do so want to try your gift. Can you undo my buttons?"

She noted his hands were shaking but he undid her buttons. She pulled the dress off and stood there in her chemise and underpants that had been made for her.

He stared at her, and she could see he had more than running on his mind. She took off her boots.

"I'll be back in a moment." And she turned and ran. The soil was fresh and earthy. The smell of the pine, oak and birch trees floated by her as she ran. This was heavenly. And he had done this for her. The light was good. She had her sneakers and would bring them out next time. The breeze swished by her as she increased her pace.

As she came on the final stretch, she could see him clearly. His eyes were fixed on her. She came to a stop in front of him. She was huffing but so excited.

"Oh, my darling Dair. Thank you, thank you."

He took her into his arms and kissed her senseless. Between her legs her private area began to throb. She was lusting after him and wanted to throw him down and make mad passionate love to him. Never in her life had she felt this way. If he asked, she would give herself to him now.

"I want you more than you will ever know. Nothing would give me more pleasure than to make love to you here and now. But I will not. When we are married, I will take you and love you as you have never been loved."

His arousal pressed firmly against her body.

"I am sorry if..."

He lifted her chin and kissed her again but gently.

"Do not apologise, my dearest. Know I want you. You are the greatest gift. I will open you on our wedding night. I love you."

He loved her and wanted to wait till they wed. She placed her dress over her head. He did up her buttons and kissed her on her neck. He lifted her up and placed her in the curricle and helped her put on her boots. Her throbbing would not stop. It was not going to stop until they married. No doubt this was not the man she first thought he was. Oh, she loved him.

They headed back for the house. She snuggled into his body, grateful for the time she was having with him. His love for her and his wanting her to be his wife. She wanted it to go on forever. Could this dream last? She closed her eyes and hoped so. She wanted to be in his bed forever.

14

WHAT A WEEK

Tea was brought to her as she sat up in bed. The curtains were open and every muscle in her body was telling her they were not getting up. She was sore from head to foot. Glenna came in and sat at the end of the bed with her cup in hand.

"Being a bit lazy this morning."

"Every muscle in my body is telling me to go back to sleep."

Glenna laughed.

"Have pity, please."

"Well, you insisted to learn to ride."

"I really don't regret it. Just wasn't expecting to feel so very old."

Glenna laughed. "You will feel better. But that's why I use the shanks pony."

"Oh yes, you prefer to walk or take a carriage."

"It is more ladylike I will admit..."

"Well, I have no regrets. Watching Dair ride is wonderful, and I want to join him in the exercise."

"Then for the time being it will be aching muscles."

"I am now prepared for the sacrifice, despite the pain."

Both ladies laughed.

"Today we will ride again, and I will hope the muscles will learn to live with it. He has arranged afternoon tea down by the lake. I assume we will walk there."

"And are you happy in your discussions?"

"Definitely. In fact, I am loving my time here in the past. Perhaps I might just stay. If what I feel for Dair is real..."

"That would be wonderful."

"You wouldn't mind?"

"Of course not. What makes you think I would?"

"I don't want to step on toes. You are mistress of the house."

"Only because you and Dair haven't married yet. If it is what you both plan, I will gladly step aside. I might go to the future to decide what I want in life."

"This all seems too good to be true. Us falling in love so quickly. I'm uneasy. It's as if I am waiting for the hammer to fall." She blushed and lowered her head.

"What do you mean?"

"I feel like something is coming, something that will upset this wonderful life we are creating. Perhaps his or my feelings might change."

"Dearest Molly, I do believe you are over thinking the situation. I know it is hard for you to believe that you could be happy after all the tragedy you have experienced. But you can. Life can be good, and you can be part of it."

"I never was a pessimist. I used to love the changes life threw at me. But I don't want change now. I want this. I want Dair. I need him. Do you understand?"

"I do and I am sure you will have it. Now dress and come down to breakfast."

She put down her cup and tried to move.

"Ohhhhh." She groaned. "That does not feel good."

Glenna laughed and left the room.

She walked gingerly into the breakfast room and saw the man who had captured her imagination and wanted her to stay. He stood and made his way to her and kissed her on her cheek.

"I understand your muscles are yelling at you."

She looked over to Glenna and smiled. "That is an apt description."

"I thought so. But do not worry, my dearest. It is very normal for first time riders to feel this way. I suggest we walk somewhat today to allow your muscles some time off from screaming at you."

"Perhaps, but movement will loosen the tightness. I might have another run."

She watched him swallow and give her a 'yes please' grin. He gave a little cough.

"Then I suggest a leisurely stroll after breakfast."

"Agreed."

He escorted her to the table and pulled out a chair for her.

She lowered herself into the chair and let out a long and painful sound. She looked up at her hero who reached down and kissed the top of her head.

"I thought after a week of riding the pain might ease."

"I think you will see it will improve from here on. Your body is adjusting." He sat in the seat next to her. "A week, I might add, I do not want to stop. Are you still interested in accompanying me as I move around the estate doing my jobs?"

"Definitely. If I plan to stay, then I need to know what is going on. I have loved the week you have given me."

"Well, this morning I will meet with Mr. Kalen, and I would like you to meet him."

"That reminds me," interrupted Glenna. "I told Mr. Kalen about your father and the man was distinctly disturbed by his name and yours for that matter."

"Why? I can mean nothing to him. After all he is not from the future, is he?"

"I doubt it very much and he has lived here for well over twenty years and has never ever mentioned the fae or even hinted at my mother's ancestry."

Glenna looked at her. "I do not like it. He seems to be avoiding me since we spoke. He always finds an excuse to be somewhere else."

"Do not imagine what is not there, sister. The man has a large estate to manage and has a great deal of work to be done before the winter comes. He probably did not want to disturb you."

"I am not so sure."

"Dair, Glenna has a sense for these things. When I meet, I will watch him carefully to see if I too can make out anything. You can be with us when we meet if you like. Can't she, Dair?"

"Of course, but I am sure all will be well."

He drank from his coffee. She looked at Glenna who was not smiling. Concern was written on her face. Concern. Suddenly the concern Glenna felt had become part of her. There was something wrong and she too could sense it.

What the hell was going on? Was this the hammer?

The walk was a chance to discuss the wonderful time they had. And he wanted to hear her thoughts.

"I am sure that my aches and pains with riding will diminish."

"I am sure also. Have you enjoyed all we have done this past week?" He patted her hand which was looped around his arm.

"Oh, where do I start? I have loved every minute. Riding with you. Going into Aberlour. Our long and fruitful walks and discussions. Picnics. I am sure there will not be too many glorious days of summer left to do that. Then cooking in the kitchen with Mrs. Gillies. And you watching and laughing at me."

"With you my dear, not at you." He took her hand and gave it a little squeeze.

"That's true. The extensive tour of the house with the housekeeper, Mrs. Boyce. What else. Our ride in the carriage to see the distillery. That was heaps of fun. We have had two walks in the rain, which I loved. Our quiet afternoons in the library reading and you massaging my aching feet. The gift of my running track. The longing in your eyes when I had finished my run. Everything has been exceptional and marvellous."

He stopped walking and took her into his arms. He remembered the wanting, watching her run, and wanting to make love to her beautiful body.

"Are you happy?"

"Very, Dair. Being with you makes me happy."

He leaned down and kissed her sweet warm lips. Never had he craved a woman as he wanted her. Feeling her in his arms only made him want her more.

"Dair, my dear?"

"Yes, my darling?"

"I do believe you are aroused."

"Does that shock you, madam?"

"No, it's another thing I love."

He kissed her again and deeper than before. He wanted her as his wife and the sooner the better. He would never compromise her.

"I think we had better stop before I take you here and now."

"Promises, promises."

"A promise I cannot wait to fulfil."

They continued their walk.

They made their way to Dair's study. Glenna was glad that Molly had suggested she be there to see Mr. Kalen's reaction when he finally met Molly. Dair was at ease and thought all the fuss was nonsense.

They did not have to wait long as Mr. Kalen was standing in the study waiting for his laird.

She seated herself down near Dair's desk. Her eyes alighted on Mr. Kalen.

There was a hint of recognition between them. So strange she should feel that of a man she had only seen at a distance. But it was there. Recognition. What did that mean? He was well dressed. His hair greying at the temples. His hair was still wavey as it was in the photo that she had of him. The only photo. Her father? Wishful thinking. Her mind wanting to make scenarios of why her father left. She was thinking he could be related to her father who was yet to be born.

He kept staring at her. He could not stop staring at her, she noticed.

Now she was uncomfortable. Bewildered he would see her, know her in any way at all. She shivered. Shudders running through her. Someone walked over her grave. That is what her Scottish grandmother use to say when she was small. Her mother's mother. She had stayed close to them until she had died when she was ten.

"Mr. Kalen, may I introduce you to Miss Molly Grace."

She stood as Mr. Kalen came and stood before her. She curtsied and he bowed.

"Very pleased to meet you, miss."

His eyes never turned away from her.

She sat down and he returned to stand before the laird's desk.

"Miss Grace's father was a Sen Kalen."

"I am Sen Kalen. I am Molly's father."

"I beg your pardon?" She stood.

Her world was spinning out of control. She glared at the man who she loved as he grabbed the man who had declared he was her father, around his collar. Then blackness rose from the floor and took her in.

15

BACK TO THE PAST

She heard the voices but did not make sense of where she was or whose voices she was hearing. She was laying down. But where? There was a slight buzzing in the air and smell of pine. Her head was resting in a lap, but whose she could not tell. The jumbled words slowly began to take shape and she understood them.

"I am sorry sir, but it is true. I had no idea she would react like this."

"But you cannot be her father. It is impossible."

"But I am. There is more she will need to hear."

She pulled herself into an upright position but leaned back into the body of her beloved who had been cradling her head in his lap. She was on the floor of Dair's study, and he was on the floor sitting with her. This was nuts. That was all that kept leaping into her brain.

This was nuts. Impossible.

"I won't believe you until you can give me some proof." She glared at him. Her so-called father.

"I will give you our complete history if you listen to me, Molly."

"Don't call me Molly. I don't know you."

"But I know you. You were born on March twenty-third, 1993. Your sister Skye was born three years earlier on September fifteenth. Your mother was Carina Grace, born in Melbourne. Her birthday was December fifth. And we married on January eighteenth, 1988. I came back in time in 1996 on the orders of the fae."

"I don't believe you."

"But it is true, Molly."

Her head was ready to burst. "Do not call me Molly." She placed her hands over her ears and pressed hard trying to block the buzz that seemed to be taking over her brain.

"I want you to know the truth. I want you to understand you are being manipulated because you are fae."

"I am not fae. You are mad. Go away and leave me alone."

"I will leave but I am ready to talk with you when you are ready to listen."

She watched him bow and leave the room. Her head hurt more than it ever had. Was this what it was like before one had a stroke? She could imagine it just might be like this.

The voices around her were distant again and she closed her eyes. The room had started to spin. The only thing that felt secure were the arms wrapped around her. Alasdair.

The darkness enveloped her. And she wanted to stay in this void forever. She didn't want to think about her mum, her sister, Flora, or the past. Her past. She wanted to live in the dark place and not face truth or lies. Her dreams with Dair were unravelling.

This is the hammer.

She heard his voice, trying to bring her out of the void, out of the place giving her peace.

"Open your eyes, my love, and speak to me." He repeated.

"I don't want to."

"Please my darling. Listen to me."

She kept her eyes closed and listened to the beat of his heart, tapping on her back.

"I'm listening."

"We need to talk about this. But I want you to know I am here to stand beside you. Or sit beside you. We will face this together. Do you understand? Together."

"I hear you."

"We are both here." She heard Glenna add.

Slowly she opened her eyes. The room was no longer spinning. She saw Glenna staring at her.

She sat up straighter and turned to look at Alasdair.

"I don't know what to think. He is saying he is fae. If that is the case, then Skye and I are fae. Isn't that, right?" She looked at Glenna who nodded. Glenna kneeled in front of her and took her hand.

"This is nuts, Glenna." She began to weep. Deep and mournful sounds exited her chest.

Glenna stood and went and pulled the bellpull. She heard Glenna's voice asking for tea to be brought. She also went to the sideboard and poured a whisky which she brought to her and encouraged her to drink.

The golden liquid slipped down her throat and penetrated every part of her ridged body. His arms were still holding on to her, keeping her from sliding into oblivion. This was momentous. No overreaction here. Her life had taken a detour and had come totally from left field. She believed in the fae and had trusted them to look after her in the past. Nothing was even hinted at that she would be fae herself. Who and what could she believe?

"Molly, I know this is a shock, but we need to find out what is true. Do you want me to talk to Mr. Kalen or do you want to?"

Molly studied the concerned look on her friend's face. Glenna was fae. She knew and was wise in her gifts and the use of them. But was this why they had become friends? Because of fae blood flowing through her body? She knew her father had been standing in front of her before he had spoken the words. There was no way anyone would have known her birthday let alone her mum's and Skye's. Not here in the past with dates yet to happen.

"I know I need to speak with him. But not yet. Can I just be with you both and think before I face the doom he brings."

The hammer has fallen.

Dair squeezed her gently and whispered, "This is not doom. This is us, heaven here on earth. We must face what is coming but together."

She again turned to look into his eyes. "You will love me even if I am fae?"

"I have loved my sister and my mother. I have every intention of loving you."

She thought she might have smiled but was not sure. The footman came in with the tea and she sat up ready to face what was ahead. She stood and seated herself in the chair. Alasdair helped her. He brought another chair next to her and sat down. He took her hand and held it tightly. And Glenna sat opposite to her. God bless whisky and the love of a Scotsman.

She held onto Alasdair's hand and would not let go. They had spoken for hours. The what if's and could be's. Over and over. But it did not change the state of affairs. She had to sit down and talk with her father. So, after a late luncheon, they went to the drawing room to sit and wait for her father's arrival.

Alasdair was true to his word. He stayed by her side and held her hand. He made no indication he would leave her alone. When she wanted to freshen up, he waited in her bedroom until she was ready.

The knock at the door drew her attention back to the here and now.

"Enter." Dair said the word and squeezed her hand ever so gently.

Sen came in and stood before him.

"Please sit down, Mr. Kalen." And Glenna directed her arm to the chair in front of the chaise the three of them sat on.

He was looking directly at her but waited to be addressed. Molly closed her eyes and then looked at him again. He neither smiled nor frowned. His emotions were very much intact. Unlike hers which were still reeling.

"I have accepted the fact," she began, "you are my father. I want to ask questions and I would like the answers given with no explanation, just answers. When I have finished you can tell me anything else you might think is relevant." She even sounded angrier than she had intended.

He nodded.

"Are you fae?"

"I am."

"Did you love my mother?"

"Deeply. More deeply than you would ever know."

She closed her eyes. "Please do not elaborate. You say the fae told you to leave us, my mother, sister, and me."

"Yes."

"Did you want to?"

"No. I had made a new life."

"Now you can be specific. Why did the fae want you to leave?"

"I was the son of Queen Sebille. She had made a ruling that no fae were to link themselves with mortals. This had never taken place before. We were always encouraged to mix with the mortal world. I had already met your mother and we were travelling together around the world. The queen had called me home to tell me I would be cast out of the fae if I married your mother."

"And you did, marry I mean."

"Yes, I loved Carina."

"Okay." What should she ask next? She looked at his features and they had changed. He was sad. He was not trying to hide it.

"Then why did you leave us."

"A fae guardian came to see me when you were a baby. They told me Carina was also fae, but she did not know. I had sensed power in her but had no idea she was fae. I believed her to be mortal. Some mortals have power. The guardian said she had been given to a mortal family to raise, to protect her from members of the fae royalty wanting her dead."

"Why did they want my mother dead?"

"Because she was the rightful princess. She was a daughter of the Celestas. The family my mother had succeeded from. There were no legitimate heirs."

"What do you mean, legitimate?"

"Your mother was fae but from a mortal father and a fae mother."

"Part fae, you mean?"

"Yes."

"I am not sure I understand and who are the guardians?"

"Guardians are the fae who monitor all the fae world to be sure they are doing no harm to the mortal world. A part fae individual can join the fae world if they wish or stay in the mortal world. I had chosen the mortal world but because I had married a fae, unknowingly, I had placed both worlds in jeopardy. To stop the worlds self-destructing I left and travelled in time to stay in the mortal world but in another time. I did not want to return to the fae world."

"Is it true the worlds could self-destruct?"

"Yes, if Carina and I stayed together. The guardians cannot lie. So, I left."

Glenna had been silent through his explanation, but now she spoke up.

"Had you doubted your mothers right to the throne?"

"Yes, many fae had. I had no intention of being an heir or any of my children to be heirs. So, I joined the mortal world."

Molly shook her head. "But you were fae and so was my mother. Didn't you want to be with your own kind?"

"I came here after I had discussed the situation placed before me by the guardian. I sought out friends in the fae world who I could trust. They told me the guardian had been sent by my mother to ruin the chances of any children of mine taking over the royal line. You see, I am her only child. My father was the previous king, a Celeste."

"I am really finding this hard to believe. I have only just accepted the fae were real and now you are telling me that I am fae and a pure blood if my mother was fae too."

Dair had been silent and holding on to her, tightly. In a low and menacing voice, he finally spoke. "Molly is staying here."

It was a true statement. She had no intention of going back to the future or leaving Dair. Her doubts were gone. She loved this man more than anything else on earth.

"I know," her father added. "That is why I am here. I will be your guardian if you decide to stay. And you will stay."

"Yes, I will. But not because you say I will but because I love Dair. Why am I being made to feel decisions are being made for me instead of me making my own?" She stood up. "I need to think on these things."

She turned to face Dair. "I will go to my room for a while. I need to be alone."

He stood, hugged her and she left.

16

WHAT IS REALLY GOING ON?

Molly lay on her bed looking at the ceiling. She kept going over the things her father had revealed. She understood what he had said but the truth was too hard to accept. She closed her eyes, but the dark was not where she wanted to be. Not anymore. She sat up and went to sit by the window where she would gaze out at the tranquil world she had come to love.

One of the stable boys was walking her horse, Greta, around the green space near the castle. She watched her beloved horse, as if time had stood still. She had no idea how long she watched but it was the only scene giving her any comfort.

What was she to do?

It was a question she didn't know how to answer.

Despite wanting desperately to follow his beloved to her room, he also wanted her to have some time to think. And he wanted to ask more questions of the man before him.

"I would like to ask you more questions."

"As would I." Glenna added.

"Please Sen, sit down." Alasdair motioned to the chairs, and he also came toward them to sit. Glenna went to his desk and sat in the big chair. She picked up a pencil and began to write on the paper he had on his desk. He brought his attention back to Sen Kalen seated in front of him.

"Why have you not revealed your story to us before now?"

"Sir, you have only come to accept your own story in the last year. Your mother knew before she..."

"I understand."

"Well, I do not."

His sister was not happy.

"You knew I was fae. I did not hide it or not believed in it. Yet you remained quiet."

"Miss Glenna, I will admit my desire to tell you has been strong but for most of the time I have known you, you have been a mere child."

"But not recently. I have been working with you as an adult."

"Yes. But your brother's departure and...you are right. I should have spoken up." He sat straighter in the chair.

Glenna changed. He watched as she went quiet. Her wanting to argue had left her, as if the wind had been taken out of her sails. She was silent. He watched her as her face changed from anger to bewilderment.

"It is, as I told Molly. All of it. I am confused, for I was told Molly would come here to the past, but never believed it would happen. She is here and I am uncertain what to do next." He lowered his head into his hands. He made no sound. Just sat there.

His own mind was whirling with questions, ifs and buts. He wanted things to go back to what they were yesterday as he and his

Molly, rode around the estate on the horses oblivious to all this fae drama. He wanted his Molly to be at peace. She had suffered so much pain and he was sure these revelations would add to her already tender state. No, Molly was strong, but would she remain here with him or flee back to the future that loaned her to him? It was a question he could not answer. He wanted her to stay but it was her decision.

He stood up and began to pace.

We are all caught by this point in time. Do we stay? Do we go forward? Do we go back?

His sister came and stood near him. He stopped walking and just looked at her.

"I am going to the future. I think it is imperative I do."

She was reading his mind again.

That took him by surprise.

She reached out and kissed him on the cheek.

Yes, she had to go.

"Tell Molly first, please."

Glenna turned and placed her hand on Sen's shoulder.

"Go safely, Miss Glenna."

"I will. Thank you, Mr. Kalen."

"Call me Sen."

There was a tap at the door.

"Enter." Her voice sounded distant and raspy.

Glenna came in followed by a footman with a tray loaded with tea paraphernalia.

She sat down opposite as the footman laid out the tea on the table.

He left. Glenna stood and poured a cup of tea for each of them.

She sat down lifted the teacup to her lips, drank and let out an audible sigh.

"I am going to the future."

"I know. I will miss you. You really think tea will fix everything, don't you?"

"Do you plan to stay here with Dair?"

"Yes. I have not changed my mind. This is where I want to be."

"I am pleased. Stay here. Stay with Dair. I will find out what is going on."

She looked at Glenna over the rim of her teacup. She would miss her future sister-in-law. She closed her eyes and took another sip of her tea. She was sure she would stay but she also knew things were going to be different. She wondered if Glenna would come home to the past. She knew what the diaries told her. Well, that was not quite right. What the family in the future said about her coming back to the past. But this was a point no one was sure of. The decision would be Glenna's and Glenna was staying silent. She made no promises or declarations. Just told her to stay and she would find things out.

They continued to drink their tea in silence. The breeze was light as it drifted over them from the open window. The sweet smell of a summer in Scotland floated in the air. Probably the last of the summer fragrances. Change was also in the air.

At dinner time Molly made her way to the dining room. She was not sure who or what she would find. The room was almost dark. A single candle was alight, and Alasdair was alone looking at his food.

He lifted his head and then jumped to his feet. He came and held her close to him.

"Are you well, my love?"

"As well as can be expected at times like this. Has Glenna left already?"

"Yes. She did not want to wait." He hugged her even closer. "Please tell me you will stay."

"I love you, Dair. I know in the depths of my heart. I can't explain it. I don't want to explain it. I want to be here with you. Unless..."

"I love you with all my heart. Do not doubt it, ever. Of course, I want you to stay. Marry me, my love. The sooner the better."

She looked into his eyes dimly lit by the single candle. She read his heart. He loved her. There was no doubt.

"We will need to discuss and plan many things."

"Yes, but stay. Marry me."

She reached up and placed her hand behind his head and drew him to her lips. She kissed him with a gentle and loving kiss. She let her tongue smooth his lips and drew his mouth to sup on hers. There was longing and passion in both of them as they tasted.

"I love you. Yes, I will marry you."

17

THERE IS GOING TO BE A WEDDING

The sun was not shining as the curtains were opened by the maid. Molly sat up.

"Is it raining, Eileen?"

"Yes, miss. Has been for some hours. The few days we have had of fine weather have not lasted long this summer."

Tea was on the table as usual. She got up and placed her dressing gown around her. Eileen curtsied and left the room. She poured a cup of tea and sat down. She so wanted Glenna to enter the room and come sit with her.

There was a knock at the door and Alasdair came in.

"I hope you do not mind me coming to see you?"

"Of course not, Dair, please come in."

He came and sat down opposite her. He was followed by a footman whose tray held Dair's coffee. He placed it in front of him, bowed and left the room closing the door behind him.

"I know it is not the proper way for me to behave, but I really do not care. We will soon be married; we can be excused for wanting to spend time with each other."

She looked at him and was sure her smile was plastered all over her face. He seemed to her to be like the cat that had just finished a very large bowl of cream. She didn't tell him. How could she not love this man?

"I miss Glenna." He added.

"So, do I. We used to have tea together every morning. But I am sure she has done the right thing."

He took a gulp of his coffee. "What makes you so certain?"

"It's strange but there were things she said and did when I was in the future that make sense to me now. Because I didn't have the same information she did when she went to the future."

"Now my head is hurting."

She laughed and he grinned at her.

"Please explain what you mean. I really want to understand."

"Well...she said my heart would heal. It was a statement not a wish on her behalf to make me feel better. She knew we had fallen in love. So, my heart has healed in some respects."

"I see. She has the information about your being fae. Did she hint at that?"

"Not directly, I don't think, but the looks she was giving me... She wanted to sense some magic in me. I am sure of it now."

"It is a strange world we live in. How do you feel about being fae?"

"I am still bewildered to think all this time my father has been in the past and he was fae, let alone my mother. I feel confused, angry, even defensive of my family. I am trying very hard to keep my mind open to what it all means...but bewildered seems to fit, at the moment."

He leaned over and took her hand. "I meant what I said. We can face this together. We know what we both are, how magic and fae fit into our lives. We can face this together."

She got up and sat in his lap.

"We have faced so much already since we met. It does not change the emotional link I had the first time I saw you. We are meant to be together. In my heart I feel it." She lifted his hand to her chest and placed it on her heart. She kept her hand on top of his and pressed it closer to her chest.

"Do you feel the beat?" He asked, looking deep into her eyes.

"We are in sync."

"In sync?"

"Together. Our beat is the same."

"Yes, we are in sync. We are meant for each other." He leaned in and kissed her.

He tasted of coffee. Warm and moist. Her insides were jumping around for joy. Joy of a man she loved more than life itself. In fact, it meant everything. She had no life without him. She would stay here forever.

He rested his forehead on hers.

"Tell me my darling Molly, do you want to plan a wedding?"

"Most definitely." She then leaned into him and began a deeper kiss.

"I am at your disposal, Mrs. Boyce. As the head of the household, you know the traditions and expectations of those who will be invited."

"But miss, it is your wedding. It is what *ye* want, *ye* and his lordship."

"Well, then I am open to suggestions because I do not know where to start."

"I gather you are not a Scot?"

"I am actually but have lived...overseas for some time."

The older lady smiled. A smile that was telling. She put her hand in a pocket and pulled out a letter.

"Miss Glenna wrote me a note before she left and said *ye* and his lordship were to marry. She suggested *ye* wear her mother's wedding dress."

"But would that be appropriate? Surely it is what Glenna should do when she marries?"

"Ah that be true, but this is an unusual family, with fae connections."

Molly breathed a little easier. She now knew Mrs. Boyce was aware of more than she was letting on. Of course, she should have guessed someone so close to the family would be most aware of the fae connections.

"Come with me, *deary*."

Molly followed Mrs. Boyce up the servants' stairs to the family rooms. At the end of a hall, she unlocked a door.

"This is where we keep items that have belonged to the family but want to be out of sight or saved for another day. *Ye ken*?"

"I think so." She walked into a dark room. Mrs. Boyce was making her way towards a window. She opened the curtains. Dust flickered in the light as it danced in the room. Old furniture, trunks and books were piled up.

"I have not the heart to sort things out. But many items belonged to the master's mother."

She stood still, closed her eyes, and took a deep breath. It smelled a little dusty but not musky.

She was sure that the room was cleaned at least once a year.

She opened her eyes and saw the housekeeper had opened a trunk. She came and stood next to her and looked at colours of different clothes laid between plain white tissue paper. She stopped and saw a white item which Mrs. Boyce pulled out of the trunk, ever so gently.

It was a white dress. But so unusual. It had flicks of blue scattered on the material. When it moved the colour changed to purple then green and back to blue.

"What is catching the light on the dress? Is that a gem?"

"Gems my dear. Small bits of crystal brightly polished. It changes colour as you move in the light. Mistress Murray wore this on her wedding day. And it looks as perfect as it did that day."

Molly picked up the hem of the dress. It glistened and sparkled as she moved it in the light flooding in from the window. Little coloured lights reflected off the walls as it moved. She was enchanted. Drawn into the beauty of the dress. She had seen nothing like it before. It was almost organic in the way it moved. Nature's beauty sewn into the material of the dress. She held it in awe of the woman who had worn it. A fae who chose to be mortal. And who was the mother of her love, Dair. Jean. The name meant more to her now than it had before.

As if her thoughts could summon him to her, Dair appeared at the doorway and came in.

"Ahh Mrs. B, just the person who I was looking for."

"And what would *ye* be wanting, sir?"

"Very formal."

Mrs. Boyce grinned at the master. She seemed to enjoy being called Mrs. B.

He came in and walked straight over to Molly. He held her hand and dutifully asked, "And what are you both up to?"

Her face grew hot, and she had no doubt it was turning an interesting shade of crimson.

"*Och* your lordship. I was showing Miss Molly your mother's wedding dress. I thought she might like to wear it when she weds *ye*."

Dair moved over and took hold of part of the dress. "I saw it once as a child. Mother had shown Duncan and I came in as she was doing so. She showed me also and I was entranced by the flickering lights from the gems." He took it from the housekeeper's hands and brought it to his nose. He took a deep breath in. "Still smells like mother."

She watched as his eyes took him to a place and time she could not go. He was with his mother again and she yearned to be with him. Her attention was drawn again to the gems on the dress, and she asked herself if she had the right to wear such a magnificent dress.

"You do."

"Do what...?"

"Have the right to wear this dress."

"What..."

"You are my love. I know what you are thinking. I want you to wear mother's dress. She would want you to wear it." He held the dress up against her ridged body and slowly she started to relax. It was so beautiful and unique.

"Really?"

"Yes really. It will look glorious on you."

"That it will, miss. Here give it to me and I will make sure it is ready for you to wear." Dair handed Mrs. Boyce the dress and she made her way out of the room.

"Close the curtains when you leave, *lassie*. We do not want the sun to damage anything in here."

She was gone. Molly giggled. Sun. Not likely as it was raining outside. She went over and closed the curtain. She turned and went back to where the silhouette of her love was in the shadows.

Dair stood in front of her now and she looked up into his loving gaze.

"Are you happy, my love?"

"Definitely. Things are just moving at a very fast pace."

"Do you doubt our love?"

"No. Of course not. Loving you is what I want. But are we being manipulated? Are the fae doing anything that would place us in the wrong place at the wrong time?"

"I do not care if they are. I want you. I need you."

"Yes, we need each other. Don't we?"

"Exactly. Let's go down to the kitchen and do some menu planning."

He kissed her. Then taking her hand he drew her out of the room and closed the door.

18

HAMISH AND SEN

The morning ritual of Glenna and tea became Dair and tea and coffee. They discussed all manner of things. The wedding, the weather and family. In fact, family had become a major part of the tradition. Alasdair had written to his brother Hamish and asked if he would come to the castle. He wanted them married before they went to Edinburgh. And Hamish was expected today.

"Hamish is the youngest of the boys. His interest has always been in the trading side of the family business while Duncan and I concentrated on the estate and its expansion. Now we have put Rachael's plans into motion, things are getting more complicated here on the estate. Complicated and exciting."

"But surely I can help you. I have experience in the food industry. At least I can help with some input."

"I want that also, but I also want to be able to spend time together as a family."

"I understand." She lowered her head. It was a topic they had not approached but it seemed they would now. "I guess you want children."

"Yes. Are children in your thinking too?"

"Of course. But again, discussing all of this is so quick."

"I promised you, my love, that I would not push you. Do you wish to call off the wedding?"

"God no. It's me. So much has happened and so quickly. It's a little overwhelming."

"If you are sure..."

"I am sure. I want to marry you."

"Dress for breakfast, my love, and come and join me when you are ready."

She made her way to the breakfast room, still confused and wishing she had someone like her mother to talk to. Glenna would have filled the role had she not gone to the future. As she entered, he saw another red headed Scot sitting at the table with Dair. She knew it must be Hamish. The gentlemen stood as she came to the table.

Dair reached for her hand which she gave to him gladly.

"Molly..."

"Let me guess, Hamish?"

"*Aye* sister. I am pleased to make your acquaintance."

"All you Murray's are such big men! Oh sorry, Hamish, I am pleased to meet you too."

"*Och* you're right, lass. We are big men. Do not apologise."

"When did you arrive?"

"During the night. I got to Aberlour on dark and stopped for a bite. But the inn was full so came along and snuck in while you were all sleeping." He laughed out loud.

Molly just stared at him not sure he was joking or not.

"Rest easy, Molly dear, he stayed at the inn and came on this morning."

She knew Dair would see through her concern. She grinned at Hamish.

"You're the practical joker of the family, aren't you?"

"You have seen through me, young *lass*." He turned to face his brother. "I like this young lady. You are a lucky man, brother."

For the rest of the morning, they sat there telling the stories they wanted Hamish to know, and Molly felt were a dream. She closed her eyes and pictured in her mind what she had done, who she had met and her Dair. Her coming, her news from Duncan and Rachael. Their discovery of her fae heritage. Hamish took it all in his stride. He was not shocked or surprised. It was all correct as far as he was concerned.

"That's because of all the children, I am the one who never doubted who my mother was. She was always magical to me, and the rest of the family had to catch up to where I was. Even after Glenna was born and mother knew the magic would continue, we often spoke together."

"I never knew you and mother shared the information."

"It was more, I did not doubt. I sensed more of the magic and mother knew I did, so it seemed right to share all together. I watched over Glenna as she grew and continued to tell her the stories after mother had died."

"Hamish. You amaze me. No wonder Duncan trusted you with his future."

"Do not underestimate yourself, brother. Duncan held you in very high regard."

"Do you think so?"

"I know so, *me wee man*."

Dair laughed out loud.

"Wee man?" Molly queried.

"I am three inches taller than the laird, so he is the *wee man*."

Now Molly was laughing.

After lunch, Dair needed to take care of some estate matters, so Molly asked Hamish to walk with her in the gardens. She wanted to raise a few items with him especially about the family and Glenna's sudden departure.

"I can believe what you say about your mother Jean. I feel like I have come to know her well in the last few days. All the staff who knew her have shared so much about her."

"She was a beautiful person both inside and out. I am glad you know more about her. Mother would have loved you; I do not doubt."

Suddenly her face was flooded with heat.

"Thank you, Hamish, but how can you be so sure?"

"The magic, the fae if you want. The fact you came here in the first place. How many people would have even laughed at the suggestion there is such a thing as fae? You believed and now you are reaping the rewards of such belief."

"You make it sound so simple, so matter of fact."

"And we should. You are here. Is that not magic enough for you?"

"I had not thought about it."

He took her hand and threaded it through his arm. "Sister, you are a wonderous gift for my brother. I have no doubt what you had heard of him from Rachael, was not very edifying. He did the wrong thing, but he has changed. And if he has fallen in love with you, a stranger, and a person from the future, then recognise the gift of his love. For it is unique. He has not loved anyone for a very long time."

"I won't deny I have doubted my place in all of the events. But one thing has been clear from the beginning. I love Dair with all my heart. That will not change. I need courage to continue because things are so different. But I love him."

"Then I will do what I can to help you gain this courage. You are the perfect person for him. Now let us go and sit by the lake and I will tell you more about my *bonny* mother, *bonny* Jean."

Eileen, her maid as Dair had told her, brought her a shawl to wrap around her as she sat by the lake. Hamish had gone to see Dair, and she had remained to ponder over all she had learned from Hamish. The breeze was light but had a chill in it. The water of the lake moved gently in the breeze, but it stilled her mind.

"Can I intrude?"

"Mr. Kalen, please sit down with me."

"Can you *nay* call me father?"

She had spent a great deal of time thinking about that very thing.

"I want to be honest. No, I can't just yet and I am not sure I will. I accept you are my father. But I do not really know you. Would you allow me to call you Sen? For the time being." She said this gently and smiled at him after she finished.

"I would like that." He sat down next to her. "You sound more at ease since I saw you last."

"That is an understatement. Everything came as a shock but discussing it and facing the facts has enabled me to come to terms with the truth."

He nodded. "I am sorry I did not reveal it slowly. Give you time to absorb it. Even knowing you had arrived from the future I had hoped it was not you. I didn't want to see you in pain. I am sorry."

"Thank you. I have had a lot of pain over the last year. And I understand why you didn't want it to be me."

"May I ask how Skye died?"

She turned to look at him. The question had taken her by surprise. But she looked at him. He was sad. His eyes showed his melancholy. And suddenly the knowledge he had gained, with her arrival, had become real to her. He too was mourning the loss of a daughter and his wife and of a grandchild he never knew.

She turned to look over the lake. Then she reached out and took his hand.

"I am sorry. I should have thought of your feelings. If you didn't want to leave..."

"I did not."

"Then the shock of them dying is pain for you also. Skye was a bundle of energy. She became a nurse, just like mother."

"So that is what she did after I left."

"Did mother know she was fae?"

She again looked at him, but his eyes were closed, and she could not make anything out. He frowned.

"I told her after the guardian came. But she would not believe me. Thought I was mad. She had been brought up in a mortal family, so I wasn't surprised. But nothing I could say would get her to change her mind. She had lost any fae she may have had."

"I see."

"I stayed for two years hoping to convince her but by then she had tuned me out. The guardian returned and I knew I had to leave, so as to protect all of you. If I left, they would let your mother live. Because she did not believe."

"I am sorry I did not know the story. Mother never spoke of your leaving, just that you had gone. I didn't understand."

"How could you? You were a child and I had to go. I could not explain."

She still had hold of his hand. Explaining any of the circumstances was not going to be easy. But she had to try for his sake.

"Skye had met a doctor at work. He said he loved her, and she fell pregnant with Flora. That was when she found out he was already married. She had been working in Sydney at the time, so she came back to Melbourne. We spent a bit of time together before I started travelling. But I spoke to them often by Zoom and by phone."

"Zoom?"

"I will tell you about it another time. We had Christmas together and then I went back to Scotland. She and Flora were killed in a car accident in late January."

"I am sorry."

"I know."

He took his hand from hers and covered his eyes and wept. She allowed him all the time he needed. This is not what he had wanted and was heartbroken. She could feel his pain. So much has changed for her, but for him also.

After a time, a time of her own introspection, he asked. "What happened to your mother?"

"She went on a cruise. She had been saving for a long time. Unfortunately, it was on the beginnings of a pandemic affecting the whole world. There was no reason she should have got it. She was in the wrong place at the wrong time."

"I really loved her."

"I know."

He cried again but this time not as long. There always seemed a point when the tears dried up and he had reached that point. He sat there looking out over the lake, his head leaning on his hands. His arms leaning on his legs.

"Thank you for sharing the ways with me. It helps to understand what happened." His hand reached over as he sat up and he gave her hand a squeeze, just as her mother used to do.

She frowned. Looking at him, she could see her in his eyes. He was family. "I am glad you have spent time together," came Dair's voice from behind.

Sen stood and bowed at his master.

"Sit down, Sen."

And he did.

"I just came to see if Molly was ready to come for dinner."

Molly shivered. She pulled the shawl closer and saw the sun was setting.

"I had no idea we had been out here so long. But thank you Sen for coming to me."

"Thank you, Molly, for explaining things for me."

"You are more than welcome."

She stood and came around the bench and took the hand of Dair. She placed her other hand on the shoulder of Sen and gave it a squeeze.

"Don't stay out in the cool too long."

"Thank you, miss." He patted her hand.

"Molly."

"Molly."

As they walked back to the house, Dair could sense a change in Molly.

"Can I ask you what is on your mind?"

"Many things but a peace about what is going on."

"I am glad to hear it."

"I love you."

"And I love you."

19

BEFORE THE WEDDING

August, 1823

The house was busy, and Molly was in her bed not feeling any guilt. Her wedding day had arrived and soon she would be up and having her tea. But this morning it would be alone. Dair would be having breakfast with the many guests who had arrived. Along with aunts and uncles and clansmen from all over the district.

Eileen slipped into the room and quietly opened the curtains.

"No need to be quiet, Eileen. I am awake."

"Oh, thank you, miss. I was *no sure.*"

Molly got up and placed her dressing gown over her. She came and sat down at the table as MacGregor placed her tea tray on the table.

He bowed and left.

Eileen poured her tea.

"A wonderous, joyous day for you today, ma'am."

"Yes indeed. I hope I have gotten all the traditions right."

"I have no doubt you have."

"I wish I had your confidence."

"*Och,* miss you have studied hard and worked hard to get it right. I am sure all will be well. I will bring your breakfast to you shortly. A light one as you have requested."

"Thank you, Eileen."

The light fragrance of lavender filled the air. Mum.

Oh, how I wish you were here.

Mrs. Boyce came in with her wedding dress. Jean's. Another person she wished was here.

"It is ready, my dear. Clean and lovely and will fit you like a glove."

She went over and lifted the skirt to her face. It also smelled of lavender. It was shining and bright and the stones seemed to reflect light from everywhere. What a privilege to wear such a beautiful dress.

Mrs. Boyce placed the dress on the bed. Eileen had just finished making it and took a moment to gaze on it.

"I need to speak with you."

A man stood at the door. Mrs. Boyce came and stood next to Molly.

"Who are you?"

Molly looked the young man up and down. She had no recollection of him. She saw Eileen slip out the door as the gentleman came into the room uninvited.

"I do not know you, sir, and this is most inappropriate of you, coming into the mistress's room uninvited." Mrs. Boyce had her hands on her hips and gave no indication that she would allow this man anywhere near her.

"I need to speak with you, Molly, before the service or it will be too late."

"I do not know you and I have no intention of speaking to you."

"My name is Jake. I am a guardian of the fae as are my brothers."

"So, you are fae. What is that to me?"

"We both know it has everything to do with you. Do we not?"

"I want you to leave. Now."

"You heard the mistress, leave."

"Mrs. Boyce, please allow me to speak with Molly."

"I am not leaving."

Mrs. Boyce stood in front of Molly, her hands on her hips as Dair, MacGregor, her father, and the pastor came running through the door.

"Who the hell are you?" yelled Dair as MacGregor grabbed the man at his shoulder.

"I know who he is." Announced her father. "This is the same guardian who came to see me over twenty years ago. Haven't changed a bit, Jake. Still travelling through time making a nuisance of yourself?"

"A guardian." Dair came and stood in front of the intruder.

"You had better leave. And without my wife."

"You are not married yet, laird. And if the foolish girl goes ahead, she will lose her life."

"Rubbish. Do you hear me. I love Dair."

"I do not doubt your love Molly, but there is more at stake here than your love."

"And what could it be?" Dair looked menacingly toward this fae of doom. That's the way she saw these so-called guardians.

"Jake, you are being manipulated by the queen." Her father declared.

Jake shook off his captor and faced Sen. "Why would you say that fae? She is your queen."

"Not anymore. I chose a mortal life and I know her better than you. Did she bother to tell you she is my mother?"

"You sprout lies, fae."

"I do not. She is my mother, and she has been lying to all the guardians."

"Why would she do that when we are there to protect her. I will not listen to this..."

Three other figures came into the room.

"Glenna." Molly ran to her friend and threw her arms around her. "I am so glad you are home."

"So am I, Molly. Even if it is to only put this crazy situation to bed for good."

"What are you doing here, brothers?" Jake addressed the two men who had come through the door with Glenna.

"We are here to stop you, Jake. We have much to tell you." The taller of the gentlemen had spoken. He then turned to Molly. "Miss Molly, my name is Blake. I too am a guardian of the fae. And I believe the queen has indeed been lying to the guardians."

"This is ridiculous. The queen is honour bound to serve the fae."

"The queen is honour bound to serve herself." Her father added. "And it is about time you realised her real motivation. Herself."

The pastor stepped forward. "We are here to wed these two," his hand went out to Dair and Molly. "Can I suggest the marriage take place, and this be discussed later."

"They cannot marry." Yelled Jake. "And besides I thought you were a religious man and did not believe in the fae."

"I am also a man of the highlands, *yer ken.* There is more in heaven and earth than you will admit."

"You know nothing, preacher."

"On the contrary fae, their love is greater than your excuses."

"MacGregor, take the wedding guests out into the grounds. Show them the gardens and have morning tea. We will allow

Molly to have her breakfast and to dress and we will all meet in the library, away from the others to sort this all out. Glenna, thank you for coming home. Will you stay with Molly? The rest of you gentlemen please accompany me downstairs while we await Molly to join us."

There were mutterings and agreements as all turned and left the room leaving Molly, Glenna, Mrs. Boyce, and Eileen who had also returned, standing looking at each other. Dair came over and kissed her and he too went downstairs.

What had just happened?

"Glenna, who is this fae Blake?"

"It is as he says. He is a guardian and he showed up just after you left for the past. He wanted to convince us he was a guardian, but I had trouble believing it."

"The three of them are brothers?"

"Yes. The queen sent them out on different tasks. Blake came to us in the future. Jake came here and the other went further into the future and came swiftly back to his brother Blake. There is so much to tell."

"But where to begin..."

"Exactly. The nut of it, yes nut of it, because this is nuts and I know what you mean now. The nut of it is with Dair's diaries and my experience we were able to convince Blake the queen could not be trusted. There is more to it but this is enough to go on."

"I just want to get married to Dair and live happily with him."

"I know sister, and I have every intention of you doing just that. We are more than friends, we are family."

Molly hugged her sister-in-law and did not want to let go.

"Now Mrs. Boyce, let's get some fresh tea up here and Eileen, lets help Molly get dressed. And Molly, you will go down in your wedding dress."

Molly smiled and began to cry tears of joy.

"And none of that, Molly dear. This is a very happy day."

The library was full of males. Men everywhere. Three fae brothers, the pastor from the Kirk in the Square in Aberlour. A close family friend who not only believed in the fae but did what he could to protect the Murray clan and family. MacGregor was at the door, his arms folded looking very determined. Sen was there and if he had a sword in his hand, he would have been ready for battle. Now he had to try and get to the bottom of this.

"Now gentlemen, how about you introduce yourself properly."

Dair sat down on the chaise. Blake stepped forward. "We are fae guardians and we are brothers, Laird Murray. I have been in the future where I met your sister. With the diaries you have written and with some explanation from Glenna, I have determined Queen Sebille has been lying and trying to deceive the fae, in an effort to keep the throne which she stole from the rightful heir."

"Molly's mother."

"Yes, and her descendants."

"Molly."

"As Carina is dead and her first born, Skye is also dead, Molly is the heir."

"That is so." said the other brother.

"And who are you?"

"I am sorry. I cannot tell you as it might influence the future."

"He is my brother but his name he must not utter. I can vouch for him, and Glenna will also."

Jake however looked ready to call down heaven upon this mob. "This is fanciful nonsense Blake. Queen Sebille is the rightful heir."

"Jake, I have examined it all and gone back to the fae council who have confirmed it."

Jake looked at his brothers. Shaking his head.

"Queen Sebille has been placed under guard. She lied to all of us." Blake continued.

Jake went to the seat near him and sat down.

"So, what are we to do?" he asked. "This is unheard of, for a queen to deliberately lie."

"The council will appoint a non-family member to be the queen elect. She will look after the position until all areas have been examined and a plan laid out."

Alasdair had heard enough. He had no intention of them taking his bride to be.

"Molly is mine. You cannot have her."

"It is not up to you, laird. She needs to make the decision."

"Fine then you can leave, and we can get on with our lives." He added.

"If that is what she wants. But any offspring of hers will also need to make the decision, well at least the females."

"I cannot believe you think you have this all sewn up. What if the family will not allow you near us? And the clan for that matter?"

"We are the fae. We rule this land. Laird, you have no say."

"But I do." The door opened fully, and Glenna came into the room. Trust his sister to stand up to the fae. "I am the family fae representative, you could say, and you need to heed what I say."

Hamish came in behind her giving every indication he was her protector. Not that she needed it.

She turned to speak with the tallest fae. "Blake, you have seen the evidence and the proof of the decision Molly will make. She will not go to the fae. She will stay with Alasdair. Can we not leave them to the life they want?"

Blake looked at Glenna. "The queen has been stripped of her powers and is in the year 2098. She can do no damage. For her it is over. But we need a queen."

"But it is not Molly, nor should it be. She has not known she was even fae until a matter of weeks ago."

"I agree. Molly is my love. She does not want anything from the fae, other than to stay here in the past."

"I understand. But it is a question I need as guardian to put to her. I need to hear it from her lips so we can go and put in place plans until an heir comes forth."

"Blake. You came to me years ago and did not ask that question of Carina?"

"Because she would not accept, she was fae. She never did. You know Molly has accepted she is fae. I now have to ask the question."

Molly came in through the open door and all speech stopped. The air was filled with little lights reflecting off the gems on her wedding dress.

She was beautiful. Radiant beyond words.

"Blake?" She whispered. "Ask the question."

"Your majesty." The three men bowed.

"Ask the question please, Blake."

"Will you, Molly, become the queen of the fae?"

"I recognise the importance of the question. No, I will not. I love Alasdair Murray and wish to marry him."

"Very well, your highness. We will depart."

"No. Please stay, for the wedding. Then there will be no doubt as to the decision I have made. I do not want anyone else coming to me, to change my mind. Do you understand? There will be no more fae visits."

All three fae bowed again and went to the back of the room.

Alasdair stepped forward. "Molly dearest, will you marry me?"

"I thought you would never ask."

He took her hand and led her out into the garden. Everyone from the library followed them out. The day was cloudy but there was no sign of rain. They walked to the great oak tree in the far garden. Other guests, clan members and staff came from everywhere. In minutes all were gathered under its boughs.

The pastor of the Kirk in the Square stepped forward and stood in front of Molly and Alasdair.

"There is going to be a wedding."

From the battlements of the castle a lone piper began to play, and the sun poked its way out of the clouds.

20

A MARRIAGE NOT JUST A WEDDING

At last, he had his bride at the outside alter. The estate had no chapel but for hundreds of years this oak had been a gathering place for the clan. The tree had to be at least a thousand years old and had great significance. So, he and Molly had agreed this was the most important place for them to declare their vows. Molly had made him his own *sark*. Mrs. Boyce had helped her, but she had completed it herself and all by hand. It was beautifully made but he knew what ever Molly tried to do, she would succeed and do it very well.

She turned and pinned some white heather on his jacket taken from the bouquet made for her by the servants of the castle. Beautiful white heather. The last fresh ones of the season. All the staff were gathered watching them and all were smiling.

From his pocket he pulled a broach and gently pinned it above her right breast. "This was my mother's and now it is yours. A symbol of my love and of your part in our clan."

"Thank you, Dair."

The stable boy who looked after her beautiful horse, Greta, came up to her and presented her with a horseshoe.

"This shoe is Greta's ma'am. We have painted it white, for purity and the ribbons are tied to it so that you can carry it. The shoe opening faces up so it will catch all the good luck we freely give."

"This is wonderful, Callum. I thank you."

He bowed and went and joined the others from the stables who also were watching.

The pastor took their right hands and bound them with his then wrapped the Murray tartan around their combined hands.

"A blessing I will now give. If there is righteousness in the heart, there will be beauty in the character. If there is beauty in the character, there will be harmony in the home. If there is harmony in the home, there will be order in the nation. If there is order in the nation, there will be peace in the world. So let it be!

Our lord is here to listen to the vows that you now give. Alasdair?"

"I pledge my love to you, and everything that I own. I promise you the first bite of my meat and the first sip from my cup. I pledge that your name will aways be the name I cry aloud in the dead of night. I promise to honour you above all others. Our love is never-ending, and we will remain, forevermore, equals in our marriage. This is my wedding vow to you."

"And Molly..."

"You are the star of each night, you are the brightness of every morning, you are the story of each guest, you are the report of every land. No evil shall befall you, on hill nor bank, in field or valley, on mountain or in glen. Neither above, nor below, neither in sea, nor on shore, in skies above, nor in the depths. You are the kernel of my heart, you are the face of my sun, you are the harp of my music, you are the crown of my company. This is my wedding vow to you."

"Each of you have made your vow. Traditional words spoken in truth. Now with the rings you have the symbol of those bonds forever with you."

Alasdair pulled out two rings and placed them on the bible the pastor held open in front of him. The pastor blessed them. Alasdair picked up the smaller ring and took Molly's left hand. Placing it on her finger he said, "Our love is an endless circle. No beginning and no end. I love you."

In turn Molly picked up the larger ring, looking at the endless Celtic knots engraved on his ring. She looked at the ring he had placed on her finger and saw the same knots. She lifted her head beaming her smile for all to see and placed the ring on his finger and repeated, "Our love is an endless circle. No beginning and no end. I love you."

"Molly and Alasdair have said traditional vows spoken by many in years gone by. But they mean commitment and love. Never have I joined together two souls who have truly become one. With the power of the Kirk in Scotland, I now declare you husband and wife."

Alasdair drew his Molly into his arms and kissed her. A kiss that lasted a long moment as the guests surrounded them throwing flower petals over them. Petals of all colours gently floated around their heads to the ground, creating a carpet of colour. They stopped the kiss and smiled at each other, then acknowledged the well wishes of all around them.

Molly was elated. The wedding and exchange of vows was a moment she would never forget. They were now making their way to the front door of the house. Still more traditions would take place. The guests were calling out blessings. Even the fae seemed to be enjoying the spectacular function. The flower petals were being thrown in front of them as they made their way to the entrance.

With ease, her darling Dair picked her up, went up the stairs and carried her over the threshold of her new home. He placed her on her feet in the foyer.

"No regrets?"

"No regrets. I love you."

"And I love you, my dearest Molly."

Guest surrounded them and the joy coming from them all, was palpable. After months and months of sadness her joy was complete. She was married to the man of her dreams. A man she had no idea she would ever meet.

They made their way into the great hall where tables and chairs were set out for them all. The servants carried in food for everyone to enjoy and the celebrations were only just getting started.

The three fae came and bowed before her and Alasdair.

"We will take our leave. We will report to the fae council. We accept your declaration and wish you all the happiness in the world." Brake bowed and then turned to leave but stopped.

"You will not see me and Jake again." the unnamed brother announced.

"I shall see you again but not on fae mission, I promise." Added Brake.

They bowed again and took their leave.

Dair pulled out the chair for her to sit down.

Then the parade of guests came to the happy couple and presented them with gifts. Things for the home, food, tartans, and silver items from those who could afford to. Flowers, bunches of white heather, bottles of wine and so much more. The room was a cacophony of noise and fragrances. A collection that may never be repeated.

The room was bright despite the clouds building up through the day. After all this was Scotland. Food was at one end of the hall where many people gathered to eat and share the splendour. Items that Mrs. Gillies had prepared as well as many, Molly had made.

There was dancing. Even she and Dair danced a slow waltz as the guests looked on and then eventually joined in. The pipes were played, and jigs were danced. Fun was had by all. Glenna was never far from her side, smiling as if nothing could make her stop.

After luncheon, Molly had arranged a traditional gift giving. She had sent notes to Alasdair and left it to him as to what gifts he might give. She had spent hours in the library, making notes and double checking all she had planned. Now she gave the gifts to him.

"The first is a woven cloth that I made. Mrs Boyce helped me. It is my promise to you that I can make our house a home and I am capable of cooking and making things for you and our family."

"I thank you, my wife. It is very well made, and I appreciate the hands who made it."

"I have also made you my coffee cake, knowing how much you love it."

"This is a very special gift and I thank you."

"And I give you this bible pledging my defence of the home and clan that I am now a part of." She handed it to him.

With that statement the room erupted with cries of joy and hoorahs. For doing so she was declaring her fidelity to the Murray clan as well as their laird.

"And now dear wife, my gifts to you. Here is a sheaf of wheat. I give you this to show how I will always provide for you." He handed it to her, and she placed it on the table in front of her.

"This beautiful dagger with three gems in the handle. The gems are the same as the ones on your wedding dress. I give it to you as a pledge to defend you and the home we will build together."

"And a special gift from me to you." He came behind her and hung a string of pearls around her neck. But they were more than just pearls. Every fifth spot was filled with a gem the same as on her dress. She hugged him and thanked him and kissed him. Now she would always have the stones to remind her of her mother in law's dress.

And Eileen was right. All her study of the traditions and preparations for them were wonderful. All the promises were right. The promise of a life they would live together. She was home.

She did not want this day to end but she had prepared for that also. Soon the sword dance would be performed by some of the staff. In her mind she thought how it would be. Everyone would gather around them and sing *Auld Lang Syne* a traditional farewell. It usually was not at weddings but gathers of the clan when it was usually sung. Also, Robbie Burns had brought it back into fashion. But he had been dead some decades. She thought it right it be sung today. It was sung much quicker now than in the future. She liked the quicker version. It seemed less sad and brighter and more festive. But just before they began, her father, Sen came to speak with her. Here in the corner of the room he gave her an even greater gift.

"It is a locket containing the hair of your mother on one side and the stands of hair of you and Skye on the other." He handed her the simple locket domed on both sides with glass. Her dark hair next to Skye's auburn hair. And on the other side her mother's lock of black.

"Father..."

"I repeat to you I will be your guardian from now on. Along with your husband I will help to keep you safe."

There were tears in her eyes as she smiled at the father she had never known and who now meant the world to her along with her Dair. She missed her mother and sister but was thankful that she could build a relationship with her Da.

"Thank you. Forever, Thank you."

Dair came over to her and she stood. She hugged her father, realising he had been part of her life even if he had not been there all the time.

MacGregor was now standing in the middle of the room with a tray in his hand. On the tray was a Quaich. She came over and examined it. It had whisky in it. It was beautifully carved silver and looked extremely old. She imagined it had been part of the clan for a long time. She would ask Dair about it later. Dair lifted the Quaich in his hand and toasted to her. He leaned down and kissed her lips. They tasted of whisky and honey. Then he handed the Quaich to her and told her to down the contents. Which she promptly did. Nothing would ever taste as sweet to her than the whisky she could taste at that moment. Shouts of "Slainte" echoed through the hall.

The servants started the sword dance which all joined in and were very excited. Then everyone gathered in a circle around them and sang *Auld Lang Syne*. And it was sung fast, and she loved it. She held on to her husband knowing nothing could make her happier than she was now. The circle around them moved with them as Dair led her to the bottom of the stairs.

There they said their goodbyes and waved to all as they ascended the stairs. The wedding celebration was complete, but their marriage had just begun. And she was so very happy.

21

HONEYMOON

Molly, holding Dair's hand entered his bedroom. He closed the door behind them and locked it. It was their room now. She went over to the chest of draws near the curtained window. Candles lit the room. She could see her things scattered around the room. Eileen must have brought them in sometime during the day.

Suddenly she was in Dair's arms, and he was carrying her to their bed.

"I have waited all my life for this night. You are the only woman with whom I am equal and in love." He laid her down on the covers. Leaning over her, he kissed her lips.

"My God, I have waited for you all my life. Please take my clothes off and love me all night long."

He laughed. "Your wish is my command, my love."

He straightened up and took off his jacket. She sat up gazing at his shirt and perfect necktie. She could feel her temperature rising. She was delighted he had worn the shirt she had made for him.

His eyes were fixed on her. "Now you take something off." he said, and she laughed.

She took off her slippers. "Your turn."

"So, it is going to be like that, is it? Very well." He took off his shoes. "This could take a great deal of time."

"Yes, but boy are we going to have some fun." She took off a stocking waving her foot in front of him.

They continued to disrobe until he could take no more. "Let us get this beautiful dress off you." He helped her out of it and laid it carefully on a chair out of the way. In his mind's eye he saw another woman, perhaps a daughter wearing the same dress But, that was not going to happen yet. They would have lots of fun practicing making babies. A chuckle left his mouth.

"And what may I ask, are you chuckling about?"

"Making babies."

"What?"

"Well practicing anyway."

"Alasdair Murray. How about we start first and dream later?"

She whipped her under garments off, standing there stark naked. He whipped off his kilt and his erection showing he was both willing and able. He brought her into his arms, kissing her throat and neck. He lifted her and placed her gently on his erection. Then he laid her on the bed and began the rhythm of movement only they could perform. He felt her virginity give way. He held her close, allowing her to become used to his being in such a sacred place. Whispering his thanks into her hair, because she had waited for him. He would honour her all the days of her life and his.

Molly stretched. She was sore in all the right places. Her hand was resting on Dair's back. He was face down and asleep. It was morning. She could see the light fighting to make its way past the heavy curtains. She stretched and went to open a curtain to let extra light into the room. When she turned back to the bed, she saw Dair resting on his hand and holding the other out toward her.

"Come back to bed, my dearest."

She came over and laid on top of the sheet.

"This is so wonderful, to be here and not be disturbed,"

"That is why I locked the door last night. I did not want us to be interrupted."

He reached over and held her in his arms.

"Four times we made love. You're unstoppable."

"I seem to remember you wanting me to love you the last two times."

"Did I? Then shame on me. I am unstoppable."

"That you are my love, and I am very grateful. Can I thank you for your gift?"

"What gift is that?"

He smiled knowingly at her.

"Oh, my virginity?"

"Yes." He continued to grin.

"You are more than welcome. I take it I was not your first. You seem well schooled in love making."

He frowned. "I am sorry."

"Oh no. Don't be. One of us needed to know what we were doing. Four times. And many more to come."

He laughed out loud.

"My darling Molly. You are wonderful."

He jumped out of bed. Where he got the energy from, she did not know. She gazed at his beautiful firm and masculine body and was thankful the fae for allowing her to come here. He was for her. All of him. She sighed the sigh of contentment. There was no other place or time she would rather be.

He wrapped his own dressing gown around him and handed hers to her. He then pulled the bellpull. He went to the door and unlocked it before coming to sit on the bed next to her. Moments later the butler MacGregor and Eileen came in through the door. MacGregor carried a tray with tea and coffee. Other footman followed and placed breakfast on the table for them. Meanwhile Eileen had opened the curtains all around the room and was now taking her wedding dress into her arms.

"I will take the dress to Mrs. Boyce, mistress." She smiled.

"Thank you, Eileen."

"Just ring for us when you would like the dishes removed."

"I will, Eileen."

All left and the door closed behind them.

Dair got up and went to pour her tea and his coffee. She came and sat at the table.

"Well, my dear, you are now Mistress Murray. In charge of all you survey. And most importantly me."

"You?"

"I am at your beck and call."

"Oh. How exciting."

"Let us eat and I will discuss what you must now do."

"Do? I didn't know I had to do anything."

"It is a figure of speech you could say. This is our room, but you are welcome to your own."

She jumped up and placed her hand firmly on her hips "What the heck? No way. I am staying right here."

"I both hoped and am glad for your reply. Sit down, my love." She did. He pointed to the door on the right side of the bed. "Through that door is your dressing room. When we go to Edinburgh, we will order dresses and other clothing for you. Eileen will manage all your items." He pointed to the door on the left side of the bed. "That is where my dressing room is. You can access it any time you like. My valet, Roberts, will maintain my things. But you can direct him also. Because you are the Mistress of the House."

"Wow. Mistress of the House. It's real, isn't it?"

"Of course, my love. What did you expect?"

"I don't know. Just coming to terms with reality and letting it sink in."

His smile widened. He reached for her hand and brought her to his lap.

"Are you happy, my dearest Molly?"

"Oh, Dair, do not misunderstand me. I couldn't be happier. This, being with you is what I want."

"I understand. It was like when I moved into this room after Duncan left. Suddenly I was laird and responsible for so much."

"That's it exactly."

"Then part of what you are to do is to make this room yours as well as mine. Get Mrs. Boyce to help you. Search the house. Anything that you would like to make this room feel more like home, move it here. And the same thing applies to the rest of the house. Make a list and discuss it with me later. If it is doable, it will be done."

"I'm thankful and a bit overwhelmed."

"However, for the next few days, maybe even a week it will be what we want to do. Ride, walk, eat alone. Eat with others. It is what you and I want to do. Now, one more tradition..." He lifted the lid on the tureen. There was porridge. In the other—freshly baked bread smothered in butter and honey.

Suddenly she realised she was famished.

Molly was blown away by the changes in her life. The wonderful life she would have with Dair was coming to fruition. But it was better than she could have imagined. They had a week of doing what they wanted to do. It was the greatest honeymoon anyone could have had. Time alone, time to share with others. Talking about their future and ways she could put her stamp on the house/castle. They were together all the time, and she knew it would not always be the case, but Dair had promised they would not be far apart for long.

One morning, they had breakfast with all the family. Hamish was still at home as was Glenna. Most of the guests had left. This morning, her father, Sen, was having breakfast with them also. As he was now family, Dair had asked Sen to have breakfast with them every morning from now on.

"I am so glad you came, Father."

"I am happy to be here and very thankful."

"And what about your new family members?" Glenna asked.

"Well, you know I am so pleased you are back."

"But I plan to return to the future for a short period of time. But I will come back. My future is here."

"I am pleased to hear that. Are you able to share what happened when you went to the future?"

"I will but not yet. A few things need to be completed."

"It is all very mysterious."

"Well, that's normal," Hamish added. "It would not be Glenna if it was not so. Am I not right, brother?"

Dair was chuckling. "Yes, you are right."

"I will miss you until you return. When do you plan to leave?"

"Soon. I will let you know when I go."

"And you, Hamish? When do you plan to head back to Edinburgh?" Dair asked him.

"Well, I will help Molly make a list of things she wants for the house and then I will go and have them ready for when you come down to the city."

"I am so excited to be going. To see your businesses and all you have achieved. I have some ideas I hope can be added to your holdings. Just my contribution to the family's fortunes."

"I look forward to hearing all about them as we walk around the house this afternoon." Hamish added.

"And be sure brother, she has whatever she wants."

"Thank you, dearest. It will be measured but needed items."

"I am sure, my dear. Glenna and I have some discussions also. So..."

He stood, leaned down, and kissed her and left the room. Glenna followed smiling like a cat who caught a mouse.

"That will be an interesting morning and conversation."

Molly laughed.

"You are able to get the material I want?"

"I will have samples for you to see when you come to town. And the colours you suggest will add luxury to the room."

"It's not too much, is it Hamish? I don't want to waste money."

"No Molly, this is not a waste. The house has been waiting a long time for a new mistress. I am so glad it is you."

"Okay. If, you are sure."

They continued to walk until they found the seat under the great oak tree. They sat down.

"I will have a great selection of items for you to see at the house in Inverkeithing. In fact, you should decorate it also."

"But that is your home, isn't it?"

"No, it belongs to the family as does the house once belonging to our aunt in Charlotte Square. She passed away not very long ago, and the house has come to the family. The Square is the place you will find most useful for your time in town. But the house at Inverkeithing looks out over the Forth and is a sanctuary from the hustle and bustle of the city."

"But you spend all your time in Inverkeithing, don't you?"

"Yes. I take the ferry into the city when I need to."

"Then should you not have the right to decorate the house? Isn't there a young woman in your life who might one day decorate for you?"

He chuckled. "Now sister, do not be getting any ideas in the pretty head of yours. I am a happy working bachelor."

"And always will be, right?"

"That is right."

"Mmmmm not sure that will always be the case."

He smiled sweetly. "I don't think I can have the luck that Alasdair and Duncan have had."

"You never know."

Molly loved the ease she had between her and Hamish and with Glenna also. In fact, she had it with Rachael and Duncan too. She had a new family after losing her own. Joy filled her heart where sadness once dwelled. She was lucky, whatever you wanted to call it, but she now had her own family.

"What of your father?"

She smiled at Hamish. "I am lucky I was able to find out the truth. I am sorry my mum and Skye didn't learn of what had happened, but I have a chance to get to know him and I must admit I am grateful for that."

"Yes, it is a unique experience. What of him being fae?"

"He has lived as a human since he married my mother. He wants no part of the world he once knew, and I understand. It has taken a while for me to accept my history, but I too want to stay here with Dair, so it matters not to me."

"I envy your peace."

"We are all lucky to be here."

22

GOING TO TOWN

Early December, 1823

Molly was enjoying her run on the course Dair had built for her. He was following behind her and she smiled to herself how much he enjoyed running too. They had been married three months and a routine had developed between them. She was very comfortable and extremely happy.

Tomorrow they planned to head off to Edinburgh, so this was the last chance they had for some private time and to enjoy a run. She had been using the path ever since she was gifted it.

Molly got to the cross path and stopped. She was breathing heavy and so was Dair. She sat on the bench Dair had made. He was both proud of it and their privacy and had told her many times. He stopped too and sat down next to her.

"This running for fun can be very addictive."

"Yep, as can many things you and I do together."

He gave her a sideways look and said, "Are you complaining, Lady Murray?"

She laughed out loud. He had taken to calling her Lady Murray as she had commented Molly Murray sounded weird.

"I am not complaining. I happen to like all the things we do to each other."

"Oh, you do, do you?"

He took her into his arms and kissed her long and hard. He tasted of coffee and honey. And smelled lightly of sweat and pine. She stood and grabbed his hand. He stood and she drew him behind the bench. There she had placed a rug before they had begun running. She took off her shoes and let down her hair. Then she began to peel off her clothes. He watched her but also began to remove his clothes.

Soon he was inside her making her cry out with pure joy as he set the rhythm of their love. They both cried out as they reached climax together.

She lay in his arms listening to his mighty heartbeat slowly going back to normal pace. Oh God, she loved this man. Nothing was as good as having him deep inside her. Every thrust drew him closer and closer to her until they both felt they were one being. In the back of her head the doubt rose again. She was so happy.

What would happen to take the happiness away?

"Nothing, my love."

"Reading my mind again, are you, my love? I thought I was the one who had the magic?"

"We are like one person after we reach inside of each other. We are one. I know you. No fae could do that."

"And I would have it no other way."

"Then forget the doubt. We will be together forever."

"I know my heart says that too. But my head is waiting for something bad to happen."

"It will not and if it should I am here with you, and we will face it together."

"Yes, we will." And she kissed him deeply again.

"Love me again, husband. Deep and hard."

And he did.

They went by carriage to Edinburgh. Three glorious days alone together in the carriage. They shared and talked of so many things. Her father had gone to town earlier with some belongings for the house at Charlotte Square. Although she had not been there, she had quizzed Alasdair on what it looked like and what was there still after his aunt had passed. Glenna had gone back to the future but would return soon. On the third evening they had arrived at the house in Inverkeithing and was welcomed by Hamish.

"I hope the trip was comfortable."

"It was brother. We only had a little rain. No snow. But I can feel the winter closing in."

Molly had loved the autumn colours which had been keenly on display all the way to the Forth. The heather was nearly all brown and the fern also. But she had loved the trip.

"Molly dear, you look a little tired."

"Do I? I do not feel it. I am quite delighted. I feel on top of the world."

"Then I take it back. You look wonderful."

They had dinner and an early night. In yet another bed she made love to her willing husband. They both slept, wrapped in each other's arms. Neither with a care in the world.

All morning he had watched his beautiful wife as she discussed materials and decorations with Hamish. By luncheon they had completed all they wanted to do. He watched her carefully and noted that her skin seemed paler, and she yawned several times. Hamish had been right she was tired. But then they had been having a busy time. Travelling and honeymooning. All the changes she wanted to make at the castle, and cooking. Because she loved to cook.

Their time in the city would be busy as well. New clothes for her, furnishings etc. He would make sure she had a bit more rest.

"Shall we go now?"

"We can or if you like we can have another night here."

"I'm happy to get to Charlotte Square. I thought we might stay a few extra days here with Hamish on the way back home."

He smiled. "That is a great idea. Let us make it a plan."

"It will be lovely to see you." Hamish added. "Maybe then you can show cook how to make the coffee cake."

"I will."

"Hamish—you and Molly have some tea and I will arrange for everything we need to be packed. We can get the ferry in an hour."

True to his word, Alasdair had arranged for everything they needed to be packed. She yawned. She gave her head a little shake. Dair looked at her and frowned.

"What's wrong, Dair?"

"Funny, I was going to say the same thing. Are you all right, my love?"

"I'm a little tired. I'm not used to travelling by carriage, I guess. In my time it would have taken me an easy day to drive to Edinburgh."

"I cannot imagine how you could do it. I think the future has you travelling too quickly. Can I suggest once in Charlotte Square you get to bed early and have a long and restful sleep?"

"Sounds like a great idea. You will join me?"

"I have no plans to sleep anywhere else."

The carriage was coming off the ferry when they spoke again, she had spent the whole time with her head out the window looking at the ferry and the boats and the river and all about her.

"I am so excited to be seeing the city."

She started looking around. The climb up Princes Street was bumping along the cobbles. And the houses seemed dirty, sooty, and not as well maintained as it was in 2020. She kept looking. The city stank. Horse manure was everywhere but there were people sweeping the streets and trying to make them less slippery. Some streets were very dirty. But the city did look like the one she had known but older and dirtier. How could a city look older when it was younger? She shook her head. It was getting fuzzy again.

There were areas of poverty she saw also. But the new town was beautiful. Clean and lovely. It wasn't that old after all. The carriage pulled up in front of number 7. She had not yet been to the museum in her time, but she could picture all Rachael had said about the house.

Dair helped her out of the carriage.

MacArthur—the butler, was at the door awaiting them.

"MacArthur, how are you?"

"I am well, sir. All your belongings arrived, and Mr Kelan arrived safe and well too, sir. He is in the parlour."

"Thank you, MacArthur. And Grace." the maid curtsied "This is your new mistress."

Molly was excited. "My maiden name was Grace. Molly Grace."

She curtsied and Molly curtsied back.

"Now Grace, please take your mistress to the main bedroom."

He kissed Molly on her forehead.

"I want you to lay down until dinner is ready."

"This way, ma'am." And Grace led her up the stairs.

She had slept but was not sure how long. As she was laying there, she took stock. In her mind she made a list. COVID was on the top. She asked herself if she had brought the virus with her? But she dismissed that idea. She had been here in the past over four months and was only now feeling tired. And she was not showing signs of any flu like symptoms. Just tired.

Dair opened the door and poked his head around.

"I'm awake, darling. Please come in."

"How do you feel, my dear? You have been asleep for some hours."

"Have I really? That is strange."

"Dearest, you have not had your flows for around ten weeks. I sat down and worked it out."

She sat up and looked at her husband.

"I can't say I have noticed. Having too much fun with you. My darling. Are you suggesting I am pregnant?"

"Yes, my dear, I think it quite likely you are with child."

She shook her head. She closed her eyes and thought. It was true she had not had her periods since the second week after they had married. Since then, they had made love where and whenever they could. That would mean she had to be at least three months pregnant. She did not have any morning sickness. But she had been fatigued in the last few weeks. Noticeably. She placed her hand on her left breast. They were bigger and sore. Dair placed his hand on her breast and gave it a little squeeze.

"They are swollen, are they not? And tender to the touch?"

"Yes, my love," she replied. "I do believe they are."

"My mother was never sick when Glenna was inside her. Just tired. Is it possible?"

She began to cry. Sob. He held her in his arms. It took a while for her to calm down.

"I am sorry."

"My darling Molly, why are you sorry?"

"I should have taken precautions."

"Precautions. Do not be silly. This is wonderful. You are wonderful."

"Wonderful. Then you are not mad?"

"Why would I be mad? I am delighted. You will be making me a father. I could not be more excited."

"Good then prove it to me."

"Prove what, my love?"

"Make love to me here and now."

"But what of the baby?"

"If I am with child I have been for some time. If it didn't matter last night, then it won't matter now."

"Really?"

"Really!"

He went to the door and locked it. He came back and started to undress. Slowly, which was the way she loved it. She was turned on and she wanted him inside her. Now.

He took her clothes off bit by bit, slowly suckling on her neck and breasts as he did so. And he loved her ever so slowly. Passion was great but this was love at its finest. Real, slow, meaningful, and beautiful. Every stroke, kiss, suck, and lick were well placed and timed to help her go crazy. He was showing her with every movement how much he loved her. She could feel it. As he entered, he began a slow rhythm that sent her to the heights of mountains. He made love to every inch of her. He was delighted she was with child and showed it. Never had she been shown such attention and love. Her happiness mattered to him, and he showered her with love and attention. Laying the shadows of love, she held her man, never wanting to let go. She loved him and adored the life they had. She could feel her smile widen to the point that her face began to ache. She didn't care and closed her eyes and drifted into contented sleep.

23

A CHILD

They had promised to observe her body for the next week and note any other changes. Morning sickness however had not reared its head. Molly continued as normal, but she did try to go to bed early or rest in the afternoons if she could. Fatigue seemed to be her biggest issue. She was always hungry too. She was sure Mrs. Gillies would notice her taking food from the kitchen, soon. They promised not to tell a soul, even her father until, they were sure. But as the days passed it was clear she was with child. Her stomach began to thicken. She had no morning sickness, but certain smells would make her feel ill. Smells she had once turned her nose at, now made her want to vomit. Even saying the word made her feel terrible.

It was a Thursday, a week after they had arrived, and she was at the dress makers having another fitting. Her seamstress asked her.

"Madam, is it possible you are with child?" She asked.

Molly looked at her and began to cry. She could cry at a drop of a hat.

Boy, she was pregnant alright.

"Do not fret madam, I have things you can use to widen the dresses as you grow."

"Can you do that?" she cried. "I don't want to buy all these dresses and have to buy more for my pregnancy."

"Do not concern yourself, madam. I will also make you some dresses for your later months. We will look after you."

They had been true to their word. They had done all they could to get her clothing right. She trusted they would do so as she became bigger and bigger. When Alasdair picked her up, she was in high spirits. She told him what the seamstress had said.

"Well, if she has seen the change then perhaps it is time to tell the family."

"Okay. Tonight, at dinner. Father and Hamish will be there. They can be the first."

"Very well, tonight."

She was elated. She was so keen to tell her father, but she wanted Hamish to be there as well. As they sat at the table, she was offered a glass of wine. She declined. She had always enjoyed a glass of wine but wanted to cut it out of her diet now she knew she was expecting. She asked MacArthur if she could have a pot of tea and cup brought to her instead. MacArthur looked at her strangely, bowed and went to fetch her request.

"Are you feeling well, Molly?" her father asked.

"You're with child." Hamish looked at her smiling.

"For a bachelor Hamish, you know a great deal about women." She laughed. "Yes I am."

She was surrounded by both men, who were hugging and kissing her.

Molly looked at her father who had tears falling down his face. He was happy. She hugged him close.

All the losses she had experienced were terrible, but this promise of new life was all she could wish for. And a gift to her father after all he had given up.

Hamish slapped Dair on his back. "Well done, brother."

"He didn't do it alone Hamish. I think I had something to do with it too."

Hamish was laughing but stopped short when he saw the frown on Molly's face.

"I am sorry, sister. Of course, you did."

"Good, so long as we have that straight."

All the men began to laugh, and she soon found herself drawn in.

The coming days were a blur. Alasdair and Hamish had gone through all the saved child items at the Inverkeithing house. Hamish had ordered any new items that were needed. Dair had also written to Mrs Boyce and Mrs. Gillies of the exciting news. He thought it was better to let them know as soon as was able because news travelled faster than light in Scotland, she thought it would happen in most places. Try and keep a secret and someone always found out.

She had a number of more fittings but today she was going to pick up her new wardrobe of clothing. Mrs. Albermar had them all ready, to show her. Even Dair had come to see them all. Each was a work of art, as far as she was concerned. Anyone who could tailor such beautiful outfits deserved the praise.

"Oh, thank you Mrs. Albermar. They are all so lovely."

"You are more than welcome, Madam Murray. You will look

beautiful in any of the outfits I have created for you. I have also made this for you, madam." She handed a small package wrapped in light tissue paper.

Molly slowly opened it. A delicate cotton night dress for a babe was on top of a matching nightie for her. She cried quietly.

"Thank you, Mrs Albermar. It is sweet of you to think of my wife so."

"Nonsense, Laird Murray. It is a distinct pleasure. You have a beautiful wife."

"Thank you." Molly added not knowing what to say. "We will return in an hour to pick up the packages, if that is suitable."

"No need, madam. I will have them wrapped and delivered to Charlotte Square this afternoon."

"Thank you, Mrs Albermar." She headed for the door. "And for the beautiful gift."

"Go and sit in the carriage, dear. I wish to pay the bill."

He paid and gave some extra.

"Can you have another six nighties and baby gowns done? I would like her to have one for each day of the week. I want her to feel she is a princess after the babe is born."

"I understand, Laird Murray. I will make each one different and beautiful. They will be completed in the week. Do you wish me to send them to the estate?"

"Yes, Mrs. Albermar. That would be wonderful. I hope to head home in the next few days."

Suddenly, a scream echoed through the room and a chill greater than the coldest day travelled up his spine.

Her father was standing outside the carriage as she came out the door.

"Have you finished your errands, Father?"

"I have, my dear. I thought I might ride back with you to Charlotte Square."

"Of course. Are you well? You look confused."

He took her hand and helped her into the carriage.

"It is strange. I have had the feeling I have been watched. I just cannot seem to shake the feeling off."

"That is strange. Have you seen anything of the guardians?"

"No. I am sure they would not break their promise to you."

"Have you seen anything or anyone that might give you concern?"

"No. It is very strange."

At that moment a bent-over old lady came to the carriage door and began to beg.

"Leave, old mother. We have nothing for you."

"But I have something for you..."

Everything went in slow motion as she watched the old woman pull a knife and reach through the window to slash her. She screamed long and hard and pulled herself to the other side of the carriage.

Her father pulled the woman away who then turned the knife on him and stabbed him in the shoulder. People came from everywhere. The woman was held down on the ground. She was screaming and shouting but it was incoherent to her.

Her father sat on the ground next to the old lady with the knife still in his shoulder.

Dair was opening the carriage door and begging her to talk to him.

"What has happened? Are you well, my dear?"

That was all she remembered as everything went black.

Her head was hurting. She had her eyes closed. Her arm was hurting too. Was her father alright?

She sat up. Still in the carriage but it was moving, very slowly. Her father sat on the opposite side, still with the knife in his shoulder.

"Father?"

"I am well, daughter. Do not *fash.*"

Dair was next to her holding her arm, a petticoat wrapped around it.

"I fainted." It was a statement rather than a question.

"Yes, my love."

"Father?"

"I will be fine. We are going to see a surgeon."

"We are going...am I hurt? The baby? Dair, am I alright?"

He wrapped his arms around her.

"Shhh, my dearest. T's but a scratch."

She cried. She could not stop.

What the heck was going on?

After a time, she asked. "Who was the woman?"

"She ran away after she stabbed me, but some chased after her. It seems she disappeared."

"Who was she?"

"My mother, the ex-queen."

"But I thought she had been taken to the future."

The carriage pulled up. The driver and some other men helped her father out of the carriage. Dair helped her out and carried her into the surgeon's rooms. Her father went in one room and she another. Dair stayed with her.

"Have they caught the mad woman who did this?" the doctor asked.

"Not yet.

"Now, Mrs Murray, I understand you are with child?"

"Yes, about three months, maybe four."

"Some surgeons are using gases, but I would rather not in your condition."

"You are bloody right you're not. Use the whisky for me to drink and then use it to clean the wound."

"Are you a trained physician, ma'am?"

"No, but I know more than you do."

"Do as she instructs, and for her father also."

"But sir..."

"Do as we say."

The next few hours were the worse she could ever remember. The surgeon was a good one, but she spent a lot of time in a faint or holding on to a scream. She could hear her father in pain also. Alasdair held her through the whole ordeal. Her arm had a deep slash on it, inflicted by the queen. The surgeon went as swiftly as he dared and placed all his tools to soak in whisky. He spoke to her about germs, and she convinced him no self-respecting germ would get near the Scottish brew if it wanted to live.

Her father was weak but alive. The knife had missed all vital organs and veins. But it had pierced muscle which would take time to heal. She was sitting in a great armchair the servants had carried in so she could be comfortable. Morag, her servant in the Charlotte Square house came in to see her regularly. She would bring tea and food for her. The pain was not as bad since she had come back to Charlotte Square. One of the things she brought from the future was Ibuprofen. She had placed them in pockets etc. all over her body. For emergencies only. And she was glad she had. Her father would need some too when he woke.

Dair had been in and out to see her. But he was doing what he could to find this woman, this queen. Blake had shown up not long after they had arrived home. Her ears were still ringing from the raised voices she had heard.

She would do what she could to keep her wound and her father's wound clean. She had learned a few things about nursing from her sister. Skye would have been proud of her. Not just the way she had stuck to her guns about antiseptics but the fact she didn't scream on top of her lungs all the time the surgeon was stitching her up. One hundred and twelve stitches. Not bad. And the surgeon had done a neat job.

Dair came in and kissed her head. "Are you well, my love?"

"As well as I can be. Any news about the queen?"

"Seems she has gone back to another time. Drake assures me they will find her."

She looked up at him. "Does he? Well, I think that is shit."

Dair's mouth dropped open.

"I'm sorry, Dair, but look at what she did to *Da,* let alone me."

"You called your father *Da*."

Tears were leaking from her eyes. This was her father, her *Da*. He had become an important part of her life and he might be taken from her. As her mother and sister was. So, she was mad, frustrated, angry, and shitted off. It was all boiling over.

"I don't want him to die."

He kneeled next to her and took her other hand. "I understand. I am sure he will be fine." He kissed her fingers.

"I hope you are right."

"I would like you to go to bed. I will sit with him and wake you when he comes around."

"Very well. I am tired. But promise?"

"I promise."

She stood and gave her husband a big hug. He held her close then let her go. She turned and watched her father breathing lightly. A day she wanted to forget.

24

BLAKE PROMISES

Over the coming days her father improved, and she felt the danger had left him. Her arm was healing, and the staff were looking after her above the call of duty. It would seem they were worried about their mistress. She saw them with concern on their faces most days. They fed her, reminding her she was feeding her babe as well. And took good care of her father. Dair was a tower of strength. But his anger for the queen and Blake was evident. She caught him several times pacing the floor of their bedroom or in the parlour or library. This disturbed her. She did not want to see him angry. It was part of his nature that he rarely revealed. He was always so happy and jolly. But the biggest concern for her was the fact the queen was not yet caught.

With Blake's appearance, concern filled her being.

"How do you explain her appearing here and now." She knew the answer, but she wanted the guardian to say it. Make it real not just to her but to him.

"It would seem there are some who still see her as queen."

"Bully for them. They would allow her to kill or at least attempt to kill innocents. I don't want her job."

"I understand, Molly."

"No, I don't think you do. She nearly killed my father, her son, and her granddaughter, me. And it then begs the question, did this nutter, kill my sister and mother? After all they were heirs too. And their deaths were unexpected and sudden."

"No Molly, she did not. I can promise you that. She will be caught."

"Which decade or should I say which century?"

Blake frowned. "I understand your fear."

"Not fear, Blake. Reality. Anger. And I don't think you understand. How could you? She isn't trying to kill you or your descendants."

She watched him close his eyes.

He couldn't understand, how could he?

"We just want to live our lives." Dair said as gently as she had ever heard him.

Dair was right. She wanted her *Da*, her husband and coming children, not to be looking over their shoulders. Waiting for the hammer to drop. This had to stop.

"Go please and don't come back until she is put away for good. Do you understand?"

"I do." He turned and left.

Dair came to hold her in his arms.

"I will never leave your side again."

"I love you for wanting to be there, but it shouldn't be like this." She could feel the heat of her anger rising. "I want us to have this problem dissolved, cleared up, removed for God's sake."

"I know."

Her father came into the room.

"I will kill her before she comes near you again."

"*Da,* I don't want you to kill anyone. I don't want you to get damaged again either. I just want it to go away." She hugged him and brought him to the settee.

"Do you doubt we will have a future?"

Dair was troubled. She could see it in the way he moved and the lines of worry that had been appearing on his face. His sadness was overwhelming her. Heat rose to her face. She was angry too. How dare this woman try to stop her having the love that she had waited for all her life?

Molly sat down next to her father. Then she looked at Dair.

"Dair, I love you and have no intention of going anywhere. This is what I want. You. And the baby. And *Da.*"

"What about me? Do I come into this equation?"

It was Glenna. She was wearing the bluest of blue evening gowns. But that was not all. It was a dress from the 21st century. Molly jumped up and grabbed her friend and sister-in-law. They hugged and almost cried. She had been gone longer than anyone thought she would.

Glenna gently took her arm and looked at the bandage going up and down her arm. Then she looked at the pale and ailing face of Sen.

"I am sorry."

"'Tis not your fault, Glenna." Dair hugged his sister. "You are not to blame."

Glenna blushed a bright crimson red.

"Maybe but I can be angry, can I not?" She sounded angry.

"Of course, you can Glenna. But we just want the whole thing to stop."

"Blake has promised me it will end and soon."

"You have been talking with Blake?"

"Yes. He is in the future, trying to sort this out. I said I was coming home. So here I am."

"And here you are. Tell us what you have been doing."

"Not now. I want a bath and to change clothes. Please be patient. I will tell you all. Just not for a while."

"Why?" Molly looked deep into Glenna's eyes. She would tell all her story but there was more to be done. Glenna looked at her and nodded. Seems she could read Glenna's mind.

Glenna smiled and left the room.

Whether she wanted it or not, her magic was starting to reveal itself. She could send messages to other fae minds. And they could understand and respond. It was more than reading of minds. It was a conversation unheard by others but could be quietly heard by her and the recipient. She just witnessed it with Glenna. Glenna had much to tell but was making it clear to her it was neither the time nor place. She would wait till her sister-in-law was ready.

Dinner time was a welcomed time. Glenna was back. Hamish had come to Charlotte Square and planned to stay a while. Nodding, Dair looked towards Sen. He was improving and most importantly of all so was his wife. He was attentive to all but was clearly happier now that the family was together.

Molly was a tower of strength. The arm had been damaged and he was unsure how she was really feeling. Since the attack he had held her in his arms but was afraid to do anything else, in case she should break. It was a ridiculous thought, but he could not get away from the idea he had almost lost her. But she had rallied. She was careful that care was taken to keeping her wound and her father's free from 'infection'. She had talked to him about how her sister was a nurse and she had learned a few things from her.

But now they sat all together having dinner.

"I brought some more Ibuprofen as you asked, I can imagine you would need it."

"Thank you. We will. Though I am using for myself sparingly. It will not be relied on if I can find alternatives."

"How does your arm feel?" he asked tentatively. His wife had been angry for some days both with the events and the lack of news, that they had caught the old queen, her grandmother. He knew it was not directed to him, but he was keen to keep her calm for her and the baby's sake.

"I am fine, Dair. It hurts and I will wear a scar for many years. But I will be at peace." She placed her hand on his knee and gave it a squeeze.

He took her hand in his and gently squeezed. She was not herself.

"I should say congratulations. A babe is a blessing."

"Thank you, Glenna. It is." He rose to his feet. "If you will excuse me."

He could not stay in the room any longer. He was not at peace. For the first time in his life, he wished he was fae so that he could go out and find this woman.

He walked out the front door and across the road to sit in the park. He was angry, sad, and concerned for Molly all at the same time. But mostly incensed. He could do nothing to get justice for his Molly and he was taken aback by her anger to Blake though he could understand why she was. He had said nothing. He was so incensed that if he had opened his mouth, he would have hit someone. And of course, it would have been Blake.

Hamish. His brother knew better than to allow Molly to come after him. He stood in front of him calm and relaxed. Hamish was the epitome of calm and pure relaxation. He had never seemed ruffled. Just like his fae mother. It seemed wrong men didn't have the chance to be fae in a mixed marriage. But with his anger the way it was now it was probably a good decision the fae had made. Otherwise, a great many more fae and humans could be dead.

"Are *ye* alright, brother?"

A simple question.

"Nay, I am not."

"I am with *ye*. I do not appreciate some fae taking revenge on the ones we love."

And that was it. His brother had nailed exactly what he was thinking.

"Aye and the fact I *canna* say a word about it."

"You're slipping into your mother tongue, brother."

"I wish it were true, but my mother is fae and I *canna* do anything about it."

Hamish gave a low guttural laugh.

He looked at Hamish and smiled but was sure his face looked more like a ghost in this evening light.

"We have to wait but rest assured we can protect her while we wait."

"But can we? Look what the stupid woman did to Sen and to Molly, and she's with child. I could not save her from that."

"You cannot blame yourself for the attack. We had no idea she was anywhere near Molly let alone she was looking for her. We know now and can save Molly and the babe from any more harm."

It was true and Hamish was right. But it did not make him feel any better.

"Now come back in and ease your wife's heart. She worries for you."

"I know. I just want to do something."

"I may have a suggestion. I will tell you tomorrow."

25

DISTRACTION

Whatever Hamish had said filled Molly with hope. Alasdair had been more relaxed and less brooding than he had been at dinner the previous night. The surgeon had been to visit again this morning to examine her arm and her father's shoulder. The man had been asking many questions of her about her knowledge. Especially about the whisky as an antiseptic. She just reminded him that alcohol of any sort was better than bug filled water. Wasn't that why everyone drank beer and whisky because water was not safe? She didn't go into further detail that boiling the hell out of water could kill most bugs.

Dair had been with her, smiling at her responses. The doctor had suggested she keep the bandage off to allow the swelling to go down. But he insisted she stay indoors until he came in a few days' time to take the stitches out.

"Will it hurt to remove the stitches?" Dair asked.

"Yes, my love, but I will rest and save my energy to cope with it. I can hardly get drunk to deaden the pain now, can I?"

"Why can you not? If it eases the pain..."

"It is not good to do that to the baby. He or she is growing, and would you want a baby to get drunk? Whatever I do will affect the baby. I had some the other night because I knew I needed it to get through all the stitches."

"That is why you have stopped drinking wine. I understand. You are protecting our baby even now."

"Of course, I am." At that moment the baby gave her a kick. "Ohhh!"

He jumped up and kneeled in front of her. "Are you feeling the kick again? May I?"

"Of course." She took his hand and placed it on her slightly protruding tummy.

They waited a few moments gazing expectantly into each other's eyes. Kick.

"Our babe is alive and well. What a glorious feeling."

"It is, isn't it? We are the lucky ones."

He kissed her and then placed a kiss on her dressed tummy.

Alasdair had arranged for Glenna to stay with Molly as he and Hamish went to purchase a new bedroom suite for the baby. Glenna told them a few secrets that would help Molly once the baby had been born. With notes and drawings in hand they went to visit William Trotter in his Prince Street store.

"I will be delighted to help you. Hamish has been a wonderful supplier and your family are good customers."

"We have designs for a few pieces but of course will allow you the liberty of designing the look. We just wish to show you what they will do, practically."

"I understand. If others would like similar pieces..."

"You may make what you wish but I would like ours to be unique."

"I understand, sir. I will have each piece sent direct to you in Aberlour as they become ready and will have all pieces to you before the baby is due in May of next year."

"Thank you, Mr. Trotter. Send me the bill at Charlotte Square and I am happy to pay in advance."

"I will sir, and congratulations. The pale blue material you have chosen will look wonderful with the mahogany. Now let us confirm the list and I will let you go.

1. A day bed in the blue.
2. A rocking chair also in the blue.
3. 4-day chairs with seats in the blue.
4. Wardrobe
5. Chest of draws
6. 2 side tables
7. A cot as you call it, which is bigger than a crib
8. A crib as per the design we did when your mother ordered one.
9. And what you call a change table which will have a padded table top also in the blue
10. Last but not least, a bed suitable for the child to sleep in as they grow up."

"Mr. Trotter I am grateful."

Dair shook his hand as did Hamish and they departed.

"The furniture was a fine idea, Hamish. Looking at what we can distract Molly with. As each item arrives, I will present it to her and allow her to design the babe's room as she wishes. Next to babe's room will be a maid's room who can help her with the babe. I want her to be able to do what she wants with the babe. In her time parents are more involved with the raising of the child."

"I think raising your child is a very important part of your family. Keeping your children at a distance as some of those in society do, seems wrong to me."

"I agree. I await the day I can hold my child in my arms."

The carriage ride had not taken them long and they were ascending the stair when they heard the scream.

Both men rushed into the day room, the doors hitting the walls with a bang.

"What is wrong? Why did you scream?"

"I am sorry, Dair. I hit my arm on the side of the chaise."

"So long as you are all right?"

"I am. Just wounded my pride. I don't like screaming."

"Good to see you will come running should she scream again." Added Glenna.

"I will call for tea." Hamish pulled on the bellpull.

Dair sat down next to his wife. He placed a cushion under her damaged arm. Then held her good hand.

"I am sorry I screamed."

"Don't apologise. I cannot imagine how painful it must be for you."

"It is getting better. The stitches are tight which means it is healing well. I will be glad when the surgeon removes them, but you might not. I think more screaming will be involved."

"I was thinking of heading back home once the stitches are out. Will your father be up to it?"

"If we go slowly yes otherwise, he will need another week."

"We can go as slow as you like."

"Then can I suggest we leave two days after the stitches are removed? I think *Da* will be more adjusted by then. Now tell me about your day."

"Ah my dearest, that is a secret."

"A secret?"

"Yes. I am planning a few things to spoil you."

"But Dair you are always spoiling me."

"Good. Then nothing more needs to be said." He kissed his wife on the lips and then gave her a smile.

26

HOMEWARD BOUND

18th December, 1823

It was a week since that afternoon tea, and they were finally on their way home. Glenna and her father were with them in the carriage. Initially the roads were good enough to go at a reasonable pace. But the further from the city they went the roads were not as good as they could have been.

The first night they stayed at the inn in Perth. The second evening they stopped the night in Pitlochry. Heavy rain on the third day slowed them even more but they pushed on. They stayed the night in Dalwhinnee.

She relaxed as they travelled and the burdens that had come with her from the city were dropped out the windows as they travelled. The further she got from the city, the lighter she was. Alasdair knew people and it made her feel more secure when they were near at hand. The inn keeper at Dalwhinnee made them very welcome and fed them well. She had gone to bed early and so had her father. There were no issues, and they were well rested when they left in the morning.

Rain persisted but they continued to Aviemore. The rain then turned to sleet and eventually snow. They would be home tomorrow. She gave her father more Ibuprofen but with the intention to reduce his need for it. By the time they got home he would be not needing the drug.

As they lay in bed, she asked Dair if they would make it home tomorrow.

"Yes, I think so."

"Good, I want to spend some time with Greta."

"I do not think it wise for you to ride. Your arm is still weak. And it may be snowing at home."

"I agree. I just want her to hear my voice again and establish some normalcy."

"I understand. Did Hamish say when your things would arrive?"

"I hope some may already be there but over the next few weeks most should appear. If the snow doesn't prevent them getting through."

"Are you happy?"

"Yes, my dear Dair, I am. I just want to go home."

"I love hearing you calling Castle Buin, home. It is and always will be. I just love hearing you say it."

"So do I, actually. I have never ever felt so at home as I do there. It is getting colder the further we go north."

"It is December already and the snow is late this year."

"Is it normally snowing by now?"

"Definitely. Home may already be white. I am surprised there was no snow on the road till this afternoon. But then the rain would have seen to that."

"We don't have a lot of places with snow in Australia. Summer is the season we have plenty of."

"Well, this will be a cold winter and long. Snow may well cover the ground till March or later."

"So that will prevent many people travelling. Will Hamish come for Christmas?"

"You mean Yule time? We Scots don't do much for Yule time. We celebrate Hogmanay, or new year's. That is a very big celebration."

"Well, I won't have time this year but next year watch out, Christmas will be big."

He laughed. "Anything you want, my dear."

They finally made it home the next day. It seemed talking about the snow made it happen. It had snowed overnight. The drifts were light, but everyone was glad to get out of the carriage and into the warm sitting room at the castle.

"Mrs. Gillies and Mrs. Boyce, how lovely it is to see you."

"And you, ma'am. Congratulations on expecting a child."

"Thank you, Mrs. B." Dair added. "Right now, can you arrange a bath for your mistress. I would like her to rest. We will talk in the morning."

"Thank you, Dair. I am weary." She took off her cap and dragged her feet across the tiles.

"I thought as much. Hop into bed when you have bathed. I will have a light meal brought to you."

"Thank you, dear."

She made her way up the stairs to her dressing room where a bath was slowly being filled. She took her time to disrobe, waiting for the bath to be filled. But there was an ache in her heart. Something she found hard to put her finger on. She gazed out the window and watched the dark clouds roll in, promising more snow. It also promised her a feeling of doom that she could not shake. She pulled the bellpull and Eileen appeared at her door.

"Hello Eileen. It is good to see you and be home."

"And you, ma'am. Congratulations on the bairn. May I be so bold as to ask how your arm is doing?"

"Much better now the stitches are out. Do we have a cream I can rub on the scar to keep it soft? I want to avoid a thick scar if I can."

"I am sure Mrs Gillies has some of her lavender cream that she uses. I am sure that could be beneficial for you."

"Thank you, Eileen. One more question? Have any new staff started in the house since we have been away?"

"Yes ma'am. Two young ladies in the maid's positions and an older lady in the kitchen. And one man in the stables."

"Thank you, Eileen. Can you ask Master Alasdair to join me, please?"

"Yes ma'am." And she left the room.

The heaviness and dread had been creeping over her since she came home was heightened. She paced the room waiting for Dair to come. She only waited a few minutes.

He entered. "What is it, dearest?"

"I feel there is a shadow hanging over us. Did you know we have new staff?"

He took her into his arms. "Do not fret, my dear. That is very normal. Staff come and go. But it will be people that are known to us."

"It does not feel right. I want a footman outside father's room and my dressing room if you are not with me. Do you understand?"

"Hush, my love. Do not *fash.* I will do whatever you want if it will help you to relax. Now slip into your bath. I will stay with you.

I will ring for Roberts, and he can arrange for a footman to stay close to your father."

"I am concerned for her, Glenna."

"You have to see it from her point of view, Dair. She has been attacked by a stranger, as has her father. Though Sen knows what the queen looks like, Molly does not remember her attacker. It happened so quickly. Perhaps I should introduce Sen to the new staff and see what the reaction is."

"Perhaps it is wise to do so. Molly seems to be on tenterhooks."

"I think it is understandable. If it gives her peace, I will do whatever she wants."

"As will I. I do not like seeing her like this. She is growing as the babe gets bigger. And I know she does not want to do anything that might risk the bairn."

"I know what Rachael was like when she was pregnant."

"That's right you do. Is Molly behaving in a similar way?"

"The situation is very different, but tears are the most common thing. Either of them can start crying at the drop of a hat. Rachael said it was hormones. Something in the blood that changes when you are expecting a child."

"Then we just need to watch her and do whatever makes her comfortable. I do not want her to be suspicious of the staff who love her."

"I think you are right."

27

HOGMANAY

Christmas came and went with little mention of it. Molly remained on tenterhooks. But the castle was alive with activity as they prepared for Hogmanay. The traditions were new to her, and with the many visitors around the estate no trouble would surely occur. She wanted things to be right for her and Dair and in the nursery. Mrs Boyce said it was because she was 'nesting'. She did not doubt the dear lady.

Molly liked the term. She did want to make things right in her 'nest'. The chairs Dair had ordered for the nursery arrived a few days after they got home. She loved the feel of the mahogany, and the pale blue material was so light. It made the room seem tranquil. She often found herself sitting in the room, on one of the chairs, thinking about the baby and the changes he/she would bring.

The best tradition for Hogmanay was the cleaning. The whole house had to be cleaned from top to bottom. She helped Mrs Boyce to organise this. She was sure her wanting to nest only added to the desire to clean. Windows, cupboards, wardrobes, the kitchen, dressing rooms. Everything was scrubbed or polished. She was not opposed to sorting a draw or two out. When the dear lady would let her. And she loved how everything sparkled.

"So, the house or castle if you prefer is looking brilliant. Is it not?"

"It would seem, dear Molly, that you have taken to Hogmanay like..."

"A duck to water. Yes, I have been reading up on the traditions and Mrs Boyce has filled me in on all the traditions that are common in the castle. I must admit I like the whole idea of it."

"Well, I have done my part too. As the eve is tomorrow, I have made sure all our debts have been paid. And many of the tenants are doing the same. All the furniture for the nursery is paid in full and will be coming to us over the coming months."

"It is a lovely gift. I am looking forward to seeing all you have chosen."

"My dear, I wanted these things for you. Now let us go for a walk. It isn't snowing, at the moment. Might be the last chance for a while to get out."

In the foyer they bundled into coats and boots. He handed her gloves to her. The snow had been falling for some weeks now and was thick on the ground. Molly loved to walk even in the cold and snow. The layers of glowing white draped over the scenery in an unfamiliar way. It was her first snowy winter but one that would stay with her forever. It was a new experience but a welcomed one.

"I have arranged the fires to be doused and each fireplace cleaned by ten o'clock tomorrow evening. Do you know why the ash needs to be removed and no fires lit again till after midnight?"

"I understand it is to signify a clean sweep of the old year and clean welcome to the new year. If it has any deeper significance, I am not aware of it."

"That idea gives me joy. I like it. Although the last year saw us meet and marry some aspects have not given me joy."

He stopped and held her in his arms. "I am aware of it, my dear and want the new year to give you fresh promise."

"Now, tell me of the first foot." They walked on.

"Another tradition with superstition attached to it. As the bells toll at midnight, we will welcome friends and strangers over our threshold. But the first one is usually a man, tall with dark hair. He is known as the first foot. I am not exactly sure why but some say it was when the Vikings came. They were blond and would kill and ransack a village. So, a man with black hair, who brings gifts is what the people wanted to see. Also, it means a year of good luck and prosperity."

"Wow. But how can you be sure to have someone with black hair crossing first."

"Well, it should be a stranger or someone, a friend, who was not in the house before midnight on that day. Most people arrange for a friend to do the task. And I believe Mrs Boyce has arranged a relative of hers to be the first."

"It amazes me. But I think it a wonderful tradition. I will watch with interest as to who it is. Will we have other guests?"

"Yes, my dear. All our staff and tenants will come. Hamish should arrive then also. He would not dare be here before midnight. We will gather around the big clock in the foyer and listen with heads bowed until the clock strikes twelve. I will then open the door to our guests and visitors."

"I am so looking forward to it, Dair."

"As am I, Molly. I want our coming year to be filled with joy."

They stopped and hugged each other again with no desire to let go.

When she woke the next day, tea was already set on the table and Dair was in his dressing gown looking out the window and the blanketed scene of white.

"You should have woken me."

"I did not have the heart. You were so content and deeply asleep." He walked to the bellpull and gave it a tug. "I have just had my coffee, but they will bring your tea shortly."

"What shall we do today?"

"Well, my dearest. I don't think we will walk today. A thick blanket of snow fell overnight. I thought we could read in the library. And you should have a sleep before the evening celebrations begin. For it will go on till early in the morning."

"It is exciting."

Eileen came through the door with her tray of tea items. Her father came in behind her. He walked over to the table and bowed to his daughter. He then leaned over and kissed the top of her head.

"How are you feeling, Molly?"

"I am fine, Da. My arm is no longer stiff." She pushed up the sleeve to reveal her scar. "What about your shoulder?"

"As you can see, I still wear the sling to stop me from using the arm and doing further damage. I am amazed how much doctoring you learned from your sister. I am sure I will be fine in no time."

"Some of it is basic and I know because I just know. But so long as you are feeling better, that is all I can ask for."

"Would you like a cup?"

"Yes, if I may." Sen looked at Alasdair.

Alasdair nodded.

"I just wanted you to know that I have met with all the new staff and there is nothing to fear. My mother is not one of them."

"Thank you, Sen, I appreciate you looking into them."

"And I too, Da."

"I was wary too when we arrived home. I had the same feelings you had. But they are gone now. If she was watching perhaps, she has left."

"Perhaps. I wish we knew from Blake, one way or the other."

Dair sat in the seat next to her. "I understand, my dear. We will keep you safe. Despite the celebrations everyone is on guard for anything that would appear strange."

"Thank you, my love. I am sure you are right. Now let us change the topic. What names do you suggest for this babe?"

The two men smiled at each other. All was back to normal.

The staff were all dashing around doing last minute tidy ups. Dinner had been eaten and the family were gathered in the library. Her darling Dair, Da, and Glenna. Mrs Gillies forbade her to come into the kitchen, wanting her to rest and reminding her there were many hands in the kitchen already. Molly obeyed, though she hated being treated like an invalid.

"May I remind you my dear, your arm is not fully healed and will appreciate the rest. Besides she sends you samples of everything that has been baked or cooked for the feast."

"That is true. I guess I just don't want to sit and do nothing."

"In a few short months you will be well and truly occupied when the bairn arrives." Glenna was grinning at her.

"Okay. I get it. Enjoy the peace and quiet while I can."

From the shadows came a voice sending chills up her spine.

"I can kill yee and then yee cannot complain."

Dair was standing in front of her. Da was behind her with his hand on her shoulder and Glenna grabbed her hand.

"Come out, you witch." Her father demanded.

Sebille stepped out into the light only six feet in front of Dair. She looked regal but something in her eyes gave Molly the distinct impression she was not in her right mind. She looked deranged even maniacal. She had never judged anyone like that before and even now, knowing what she was capable of, was reluctant to do so.

"What do you want?" Molly asked.

"Your life, granddaughter."

"I do not know you nor do I see you as any relation of mine."

"That may be so but does not change the fact, I want you dead."

"Over my dead body."

"Oh laird, we can easily arrange you dead." She lifted her hand and snaped her fingers. Two fae appeared from behind her and came and stood next to her.

"Now we can make this easy. Give her to me and no one will die."

Glenna stood in front of her next to Dair. "She is not going anywhere with you."

"Listen fae, you take orders from me. I am the queen."

"But you are not." Glenna responded. "That title has been taken off you."

"You will argue with your queen?"

"You are not my queen."

"Sebille, you are no longer queen. Stand aside." Blake stepped out of the dark and stood in front of the queen.

He addressed the other two fae.

"Fae, she has had her crown removed. Go back to the kingdom or face the same punishment as the queen."

The two fae looked at each other then back at Blake. One lifted his hand to his heart and vanished, The other stepped forward. Blake jumped and had him in a neck brace in a moment.

Jake and the unnamed brother came from the dark and took the fae away.

"That will not stop me..."

Suddenly a teal blue light wrapped itself around the queen. She began to scream. "You cannot do this. I am the queen. She is not..."

The light faded and she was gone.

He turned to face the Murrays.

"She will not return. She was warned if she came here, she would be arrested and sentenced to death."

Molly stood up and came to stand before him. "And why death?"

"Because she tried to kill you and your father. The evidence against her was overwhelming. You will not be safe unless she is dead. If she lives, she will not stop trying to kill you."

"I did not ask for death."

"No Molly, but as a guardian I did. I want to protect you and the baby. I have had enough as had many of the other fae. We did all we could to tell her she would die if she came back to you. She did not listen. Her mind was not in a good place."

"And what of her followers?"

"All have seen the error of their ways and have denounced the queen. We do not look kindly to those who would damage the relationships we have with humankind."

Dair wrapped his arms around Molly. "I will take you at your word, fae."

"This is the last you will see of me as a fae. I promise. Live a long life you two. The fae thanks you."

Molly stood there holding on to her husband. "Is it really over?"

"It would seem so, darling Molly."

"Molly, as a fae I can promise you now, it is all over." Glenna took her into her arms and hugged her.

"Thank God."

Her da, Dair and Glenna wrapped themselves around her and laughed. "It is finished. It is over, at last."

28

THE EVE

She sat on a chair wrapped in a big coat, with other members of the household standing around her. It was nearly midnight. Servants and family were waiting for the clock to strike.

Mrs Boyce came and whispered in her ear.

"All the fires in the fireplaces are out and cleaned. The ashes are buried in the garden."

"Thank you, Mrs Boyce."

It was getting closer. Dair held her hand. They had agreed she would come with him to open the front door to the 'first foot'. The old year was over. The queen would not return. What joy would the new year hold?

This and many other thoughts ran through her mind. Rachael was happy with her Duncan in the future. She was here with her Dair in the past. There were many other questions she wanted to ask. Like what of Glenna or Hamish. Hamish's voice echoed in her ear.

You cannot plan for others; you need to only be concerned for your life.

He was right, of course.

The clock began to chime. She stood up, still holding the hand of Dair. Then the strikes came. One, two, three... They made their way to the door. Four, five, six... They did not hurry. Seven, eight, nine...

"We must wait for the final strike before we open the door." Added Alasdair. Ten, eleven, and twelve.

Dair place his hand on the door handle and opened it.

There stood a man she did not know. He was tall like Dair. His hair was black as a raven. He was about thirty years old. He was handsome also. In his arms he held a basket.

"I come bearing gifts, laird. May I enter?"

"Yes, you may. This is my wife, Molly."

"Lady Murray." he bowed.

"Enter stranger and take some rest." She bid him come in.

"I need no rest but bring gifts for your hospitality to me."

He placed the basket on the table in the foyer and more guests entered after him. Staff and family gathered around.

"I have shortbread. Also, some coal and wood to keep you warm. Here too is a bottle of the finest whisky to welcome the new year. Some bread and salt. And lastly..." He handed her a silver rattle. "For the bairn, who is to come."

Molly could not explain it, but joy filled her heart. She hugged the stranger.

"Thank you, kind sir."

"Many thanks, stranger."

"I am no stranger anymore. Call me Sinclair."

"Welcome Sinclair. Welcome all. Let the festivities begin."

EPILOGUE

"My dearest Molly. How do you feel?" He came into their bedroom. The air was still with a sweet scent of lavender.

"Tired but in a most remarkable way."

"I always said you could do whatever you wanted to. And you have. Thank you for my son, our son." He bent down and kissed his special lady.

"You are more than welcome. He looks very much like his daddy."

She looked down into his sleeping face.

"Daddy, am I?"

"Well, Da if you prefer."

"I really don't mind. I am just so happy he has come."

He sat down next to her on the bed, lifting his legs and stretching them out. Then she handed him their son.

"Och, he is a bonny boy."

"He is a bonny boy. I have thought about names for a long

time. I know it is tradition for the father to give the child his name. But can I try? The ones I have chosen seem, just right."

"Yes, dear Molly. What names have come to you?"

"Duncan Sen John and Sinclair. Duncan after your father and brother, Sen after my father, John as a good family name and Sinclair for a new beginning."

"I like Sinclair, both the man and the reason to call our son a new beginning. I do not want to change a thing. Duncan Sen John Sinclair Murray it is. Thank you, my love."

"This is a new beginning. We have so much love to share and children to have. I love you, Laird Murry."

"And I love you, Lady Murray. Molly." He kissed her deeply. Then rested his head on her forehead. "I love you more than you will ever know."

Drake held the hand of his queen.

"It was such a turbulent time, not just for the Murrays but for the fae also."

"Yes, it was. But you knew how it would end. Didn't you?"

Drake looked at his queen. "You know of my deception?"

"Not deception. You were wanting to protect me just as Blake your brother wanted to protect Molly and the Murrays."

"But I kept it from you."

"Can you keep anything from a fae queen who can see all behind her and before her?"

"No. I am so foolish."

"Foolish, perhaps a little. Well-meaning, perhaps a great deal."

"Do you wish me to take my leave?"

"Why would I want that?"

"Because I kept it from you."

"Do you keep it from me now?"

"No, my queen."

"And your love. Do not forget your love. You are my love and always will be Drake. You are not the unnamed brother anymore. I fell in love with you the moment I saw you..."

He went on his knee. "My love." and lowered his head.

"No, my love." She pulled him up into her embrace. "Come, let us go home."

She kissed him and the teal blue light faded and was gone.

FROM THE AUTHOR

I have loved using folk law and traditional history in this series. It has spurred my imagination. I love the way the fae have developed in the story and that they too are not perfect and can give a few bad apples to history.

Having mixed marriages was an idea which was there from the beginning but the fae blood would only appear in the females. That too was my idea and I loved playing with it. If you have loved this story, then you will definitely not want to miss the final in the series "Glenna's Future". And please tell your friends about this series.

Keep a look out for it. It will appear later this year.

And just to tempt you here is the cover...

Go to my website and subscribe to my newsletter. It is only monthly so you won't be bombarded by emails.

https://www.joanneaustenbrown.com/

or join me on my Facebook page.

https://www.facebook.com/joanne.boog/

BOTH AVAILABLE NOW...

COMING IN 2022

CPSIA information can be obtained
at www.ICGtesting.com
Printed in the USA
LVHW092323070422
715401LV00031B/884

9 780648 775935